# SAVOR YOU

NEW YORK TIMES AND USA TODAY BESTSELLING AUTHOR

## EMILY SNOW

*Savor You*

Copyright © 2013 by Emily Snow
On file at the Library of Congress, United States
Cover Design by Letitia Hasser at RBA Designs
Edited by Jovana Shirley at Unforeseen Editing

ISBN-13: 978-1490506852

ISBN-10: 1490506853

All Rights Reserved. No part of this book may be reproduced or
transmitted in any form or by any means, electronic or mechanical,
including photocopying, recording, or by any information storage and
retrieval system, without permission from the publisher in writing.

This is a work of fiction. Names, characters, places, and incidents are
the product of the author's imagination, and any resemblance to any
actual persons, living or dead, events, or locales is entirely
coincidental.

# PRAISE FOR
# SAVOR YOU

"I don't know how to explain how much I enjoyed Emily's writing style. She has a very sneaky way of telling you what you want to hear without you even realizing she's done it. Her flow is just beautiful and it's very crisp, clean and concise." – **Lisa from True Story Book Blog**

"Emily Snow has a way of keeping her books classy but edgy. And most of all *Savor You* is HOT. She will assault your emotions and your senses into book sexy overload. Get this on your TBR." –**Denise from Flirty and Dirty Book Blog**

"Once again I must say I am blown away with Emily's writing. I was a huge fan of *Devoured* and then the prequel novella *All Over You*. I love the members of Your Toxic Sequel and especially Kylie! I loved her from the first time we met her in Devoured. She's snarky and sassy and she has that take no "sh*t" attitude from anyone no matter how rich, famous or related you are... This story sucked me in from the very first page to the last. Because of the whirlwind that is Kylie and Wyatt it was a fairly fast read." – **Jennifer from Wolfel's World of Books**

*"Savor You* was a 5 star read COMPLETELY!!!! Something tells me we will see more of Kylie & Wyatt I just feel there story isn't over and I'm biting my nails thinking there might be a few more bumps for them. I guess we will find out and then I can begin this crazy journey again! This is a MUST read like GET IT NOW ~ Catch a little glimpse of that hot Lucas and OMG Cal I really would love to see his story and I think I know who I want him to be with." –**Kim from Shh Mom's Reading**

*To my readers . . .*

*Thank you so much for reading my books, supporting my work,*

*and making my life all kinds of awesome.*

*You guys kick ass.*

# ℙROLOGUE

*Seven Years Ago*

For the second time in less than half an hour, the hotel TV shuts off, and I have to hold down the remote's power button until pain shoots up my thumb to coax it into flickering back on.

"Piece of crap," I complain, flinging the oily remote onto the bed.

Out of all the places in the country that I could have gone to get away from Atlanta, I drove to Livingston, Texas. And out of all the hotels where I could have spent the night, I picked the same discount inn that I'd stayed in a year and a half ago when I'd tagged along with my brother's band as they toured a bunch of bars in the Southwest.

Of course, deep down, I know the exact reason why I altered my route and decided not to go to New Orleans. I took the sentimental route. I came to the place where I'd spent some of my happiest moments just before diving blindly into a relationship—and a hastily followed marriage—to someone I'd barely even known.

Liz Phair's "Extraordinary," blasting at full volume, startles me from my thoughts. I twist my head toward my phone, which is lying facedown beside me on the full-size bed. Scooting up into a sitting position, I grab the Motorola and groan when I see my brother's name blinking rapidly on the display. He's been calling for the last several hours to check up on me, ignoring all my requests to leave me the hell alone.

"Lucas," I answer. I pick up the TV remote and jab a button on it, muting the sound of *Veronica Mars* even though the damn television is probably going to give out at any moment anyway. "I'm fine. Please…stop."

There's a harsh edge to my voice, and he sucks in a breath that's just as sharp.

"I'm fucking worried. You and Brad are completely done, and that's a good thing because I couldn't stand that shithead. But then, you leave? And you go to Texas?"

I sift my fingers through my long black hair, letting it cascade over my right shoulder. *Why does Lucas have to overanalyze everything? Doesn't he have his own relationship with his crazy-ass wife, Samantha, to fuss over?*

"I'm not a kid. You don't need to take care of me. Don't you have Sam and Falling Anarchy crap to deal with?" Like always, I cringe when I say his band's name. It's the worst name I have *ever* heard, and I've been bugging them for a couple of years to change it.

"Are you fucking kidding me, Kylie? You're barely nineteen. I'll always want to take care of you. You understand that?"

When I grumble that I do, he adds, "Besides, Mom and Dad are freaking out, too."

I work the outside of my upper lip between my teeth and glower up at the dingy water stains on the popcorn ceiling. Of course, Lucas would bring our parents into this and make me feel worse. It's a low move on his part because he knows I never want to let them down. *But what else is new?* "Tell them I love them, and I'll call them in the morning, okay?"

Just as I'm about to abruptly end the call by flipping the phone shut, so I can go back to *Veronica Mars*—at least until the TV decides to screw up again—Lucas says smoothly, "Wyatt's worried, too."

The instant I hear Wyatt McCrae's name, I freeze. I haven't

seen him in months, since before I met and married Brad, but the mere mention of him still rocks me.

Squeezing my eyes together, I shake my head and remove my thumb from the phone's power button. *Why does my brother have to be such a sneaky, traitorous ass?* "You told him I left?"

"He was with me when Brad called looking for you. He was—" Lucas begins.

I don't hear the rest because there's a piercing knock at my door. It's rhythmic, and it takes me a second to realize that I *know* this beat. In fact, I know it well. It's "Send the Pain Below."

*Fuck.*

Well over a year ago, in this same hotel, I had Chevelle playing on repeat when Wyatt McCrae snuck into my room. The CD was still spinning when he left early the next morning, well before the rest of the band woke up.

There's another knock—the same Chevelle beat—but this time, each beat makes my heart throb a little hastier. It sends a wave of nausea crashing into the pit of my stomach. I rub my suddenly sweaty palms on the comforter. "But, apparently, you took the initiative to tell him which hotel he could find me at," I say, interrupting whatever it is Lucas is saying.

My brother makes a frustrated noise. "Now, Kylie—"

I ignore Lucas's explanations and all-around bullshit because I know it will do nothing but make matters worse at the moment.

"I'll call you back." I hang up on him before he has a chance to argue with me.

There's no winning against my brother. There never has been, and I doubt there ever will be. Since he's bound to call me back, I hold my thumb down on the End button until the phone powers off.

My breath comes out in short, heavy bursts, but I will myself to calm down as I pad across the sticky mud-brown carpet. I don't have any other choice *but* to pull myself together. The moment I open the door, Wyatt sags against the door frame and exhales. That same magnetism that drew me to him over a year ago, making me tell and show him things about myself that now make me flush, is vibrating through my veins once again.

I take a hesitant step forward despite the fact I'm not wearing anything but a tank top and underwear.

"You divorced that motherfucker?" he asks, running the palm of his hand over the top of his short dirty-blond hair. He drags his hand down his face and shakes his head to each side before training his vivid blue eyes on me. "Please tell me that Lucas wasn't shitting me."

Stepping aside, I silently let Wyatt in, pressing my back up against the wood. I slam the door shut once he's inside my cramped room. Now that I'm facing him, I try to drop my gaze to the strip of carpet between us, but he tucks his finger under my chin, stopping me.

"Ky, did you really leave him?" he asks.

"Yeah." My marriage had lasted a total of four months before Brad and I both realized how little we knew about each other—how there was practically no love between the two of us. Wyatt stares at me expectantly, and I force out a hoarse laugh. When I nod, he lets his head fall back in relief, muttering a curse. "Yeah, I left him," I whisper. "Turns out he was just as toxic as you."

Wyatt's mouth drags down into a frown. On him, even something so sour is beautiful, and it nearly yanks my heart right out of my chest.

"Looks like I'm your toxic sequel then, huh?"

*My toxic sequel.* For some messed-up reason, it fits him to a T. "Looks like you are."

He takes my hands in his, rubbing feather-soft circles on the backs of them with his thumbs as if the slightest touch will break me. It won't, and I don't miss how his eyes dip down to my wrists. Angrily, I jerk my arms away from him, crossing them over my chest.

That he would actually look makes my throat feel like it's shrinking while my heart feels like a clamp is bearing down on it. Months ago, on the way to this very hotel, I told him that I would never cut myself again, and thoughts to do so haven't crossed my mind since, not even when shit hit the fan with Brad.

"Now that you've seen for yourself that I can actually follow through on my promises, will you please leave?"

He groans, taking a step toward me. I back up until my legs hit the bed, but he places his hands firmly on the slope of my hips, wraps his arms around me, and clutches me to him.

"I never doubted you, Ky."

"Don't lie to me," I say, my breath hitching on the word *lie.*

"You can do anything else, but don't lie to me."

"Fine." He bends slightly, so his mouth grazes my ear, and as he speaks, the piercing in his lip rubs against the tiny sterling hoop in my cartilage. "I came here because Lucas wants me to bring you back to Atlanta." As he says this, his hands skim around to the front of my panties. "I came here because I know exactly why you left Brad in the first place."

He starts to slide down my panties, but I close my hands around his wrists. "I'm not one of your groupies. And it's really cocky to assume I left my husband because of you. We haven't spoken since before I got married, babe."

"Far from a groupie." A smile crawls across his face. "I'd never tell any groupies that staying away has been fucking hell. I'd never tell them that I'm not leaving, no matter how much they order me to."

He dips his head, bringing his lips close enough to my face for me to feel his warm breath against the corner of my mouth. I suck in a gasp of air through my nose, but he stops me before I can release it, crushing his lips against mine. Even though the kiss is short, it's anything but sweet. It's possessive and rough. Hungry and painful and even a little mind-altering.

But it sure as hell isn't sweet.

Wyatt pulls back, his chest rising and falling heavily. "As for you and Brad, don't try to pull that bullshit on me, beautiful. We could go years without saying a word, and we'd still manage to fuck with each other's head. So, no, I'm not leaving you."

"What if I make you?" I ask despite how the pit of my stomach curls into a mass of knots and tangles. *God, it hurts.* I let go of his wrists and move my hand up to trace my fingertips along his square jawline, shivering at the contrast between his faint stubble and my soft skin. "What if I don't want you here?"

"None of that what-if shit, Ky," he says roughly, pushing me back onto the bed.

As I slide backward toward the pillows, he follows, opening my legs in the process.

"If you wanted me gone, you wouldn't have let me in. You knew it was me before you even opened that door."

By the time the back of my head bangs up against the faded headboard, my heart is beating as erratically as it did that first night with him. He stops in front of me, his muscular body positioned between my thighs.

"What if I ask you to leave afterward?" I demand.

My fingers tremble as I drag his white T-shirt over his head. He takes it from between my hands and tosses it off the bed where it hits the curtain before falling to the dirty carpet.

"You want to ask me to leave?" He lowers his head, so we're nose-to-nose. While his thumb strokes my collarbone, he glides the rough pad of his index finger underneath the strap of my striped top.

"Maybe."

"Then, you can go back to Atlanta and forget this ever fucking happened."

I consider his words for a moment, and then I shake my head. I don't want to forget. "I can't do that," I say aloud.

He already knows I can't, or he wouldn't have come here to begin with.

He pulls my strap all the way down and sighs heavily when my breasts push up over the fabric. He pauses once, and that's only to make me a promise. "Then, you go back to Atlanta with me."

It's not until late, right before we fall asleep with our arms and legs entwined, when I ask him the single question that's been burning in my mind since the last time we spoke. "What's her name, Wyatt?"

"Who?"

"Please don't be stupid. You know who and what I'm talking about." I can't bring myself to say it out loud yet because it still burns a hole into the deepest part of my chest.

He brushes strands of inky hair out of my face. "Brenna."

I roll out of his arms and onto my back, squeezing my eyes tight so the tears don't fall. "I don't want to ruin things for you."

"You won't. When I'm with you…"

He doesn't have to finish because I know where he's going. I know how he feels because it's the reason I came to this hotel of all places. It's the reason that I let him stay with me tonight. When I'm with Wyatt, I lose myself.

"Do you think we'll be able to fix each other?" I ask.

The bed squeaks as he rolls over. When I open my eyes, he's propped up on his elbow, staring down at my chest. He touches the

# CHAPTER ONE

*Present Day*

"Good god, he's looking at you again," Heidi says in a hushed voice. Swinging her slim hips to the techno version of Adele's song pulsing through the nightclub, she sneaks a glance over my shoulder toward the booths lining the far wall.

I refuse to follow her gaze to the guy who's been eyeballing us for the better part of an hour, and instead, I choose to toss back my drink as I lift my shoulders indifferently.

My closest friend gives me a dark look. "Kylie, he's looking at you like he wants to peel off your jeans with his teeth. Like he—"

"Like he's some stranger who'll probably strangle me to death after we get back to his hotel room." I lift my hand to my throat, which burns like Hades from the drink I just downed, and rub my thumb back and forth across the delicate bones. "Sorry, babe, not in the mood to get choked tonight."

Heidi's perfectly arched eyebrows join together, but I'm not sure if it's because of what I just said or the DJ's newest choice of song, "Judas." She can't stand that song. She hates it almost as much as she loathes her ex-neighbor who played a repetitive loop of Lady Gaga on maximum volume every morning for months.

"You're so morbid, Kylie Wolfe," she finally moans, flipping her mane of loose chestnut curls over her shoulder. "You need to have fun and not think about *him* and his giant—"

"Don't even touch that subject with a ten-foot pole," I say sharply. "And I'm not thinking of *him*."

Heidi presses her purple-painted lips into a fine line, but she says nothing more. Her gaze refocuses on something else. I follow it, twisting my head a little, to take in an excessively tanned short guy, making his way through the crowd with two bottles of Shiner Bock held high over his head.

Even though I'm glad he's distracted her from talking about Wyatt, I softly point out, "He's not your type." Heidi's got a thing for ink and piercings—the more of both, the better—and Shiner Bock has neither. But then again, she did say she needed a change of pace this trip. Maybe this guy is it. "More than one beer usually means he's here with someone," I add, giving her a warning look.

Heidi lifts her thin eyebrow wickedly. "He's here with those guys." She jabs her finger toward a group of men across the club. "So, yeah…"

Before we came out to Bourbon Street tonight, Heidi and I made a deal, promising to come back to our hotel room together. But, by the way Shiner Bock's face lights up when his eyes connect with hers, I know there's no chance in hell she's coming home with me.

And that leaves me alone.

At the risk of sounding like an eye-roll-inducing 1970s' power ballad, being by myself is the last thing I desire tonight, not when thoughts of Wyatt McCrae seem to elbow their way into my brain whenever I have a spare moment to think. At the same time though, I don't want to stick around with Heidi and be *that* friend.

I dart my eyes from Shiner Bock to Heidi and then down to the empty glass in my hand. *Be the third wheel in an innuendo-laced conversation that will ultimately lead to a broken headboard?*

*Or maybe a vodka-infused drink?*

*Be the third wheel?*

*Screw that, vodka-infused drink, it is.*

"I'm going to get a refill," I announce loudly.

"Look, I don't—" he starts, but I hold up my hand.

*Better get this out of the way before I let him get too far into the conversation.*

"I don't do beads." I incline my head toward a couple of girls dancing with each other a few feet away from where we're sitting. Several rows of purple, gold, and green beads are dangling around their flushed necks. "So, don't ask how far I'll go for some. And, honestly, I think I'd better get back to my friend."

I'm already scooting off my stool before Ian's face falls, and I make a quick getaway before he has a chance for a comeback. When a large and obviously masculine hand touches the small of my back, I spin around, ready to put him in his place regardless of how hot his smile is. "Look, I'm sure you—"

But then I look up. And it's not Ian's gray gaze that's staring down into my brown eyes. These are eyes that I could pluck out of a crowd without even making an effort to locate them, and right now, they make me forget how to breathe just right. The deep scowl on *this* face literally speeds up my pulse. I tighten my grip around my drink, so I won't spill it all over my boots and his.

The sharp blue eyes glaring down into mine belong to none

other than Wyatt McCrae—the ripped, tattooed, and dirty-blond bass guitarist for Your Toxic Sequel, my big brother's band. He's the reason I came to New Orleans. I needed to stay the hell away from him, yet here he is, standing right in front of me.

I force myself to keep my voice even. "What are you doing here?"

Wyatt leans down until his mouth is level with my ear. Despite the heat caused by all the sweaty bodies around us, I shiver when the piercing at the corner of his lower lip skims my skin.

"Too fucking loud in here, Ky. Outside."

Though I know I shouldn't, I give him a jerky nod and follow behind him. Along the way, I pass my drink to some random girl gyrating her ass on the concrete dance floor, and I'm unable to stop myself from making a comparison between Wyatt and Ian, the man at the bar who backed down as soon as he started trying.

Wyatt reaches back, wrapping his hand around my wrist, to keep me close to him as we maneuver through the crowd. He doesn't let me go until we're outside and in the alley. Out here, I can hear not only the upbeat pop anthem playing inside the club but also the music from a street festival.

Wyatt's the first to say something…well, *do* something. He gives me an appreciative once-over, taking in all five foot four inches of me, starting at my boots and working his way up. He pauses on certain areas—my curvy hips, the tiny flash of pale skin between my jeans and green fitted tee, and my small breasts—before stopping at my tousled blue-and-black hair.

"Come here," he says.

He flares his hands over my hips, drawing me close to him until our bodies rub together. It's too bad for him, but I'm not having it. I break our contact, stuffing my hands deep into the pockets of my jeans.

"God, it's been too fucking long since I've gotten to do this," he says.

It's been two and a half months to be exact. I haven't seen Wyatt since Thanksgiving, and I close my eyes, letting my thoughts wander back to those last moments. For two amazing days, we did nothing but eat too much pie, listen to music, and make love. *Or lust. Whatever the hell it is I should call it.*

I didn't leave him until the morning after Thanksgiving, and I didn't feel the need to wake him up to say that I was going. It seemed like we had already said plenty. The night before, I'd told him I loved him, and he had simply stared at me—blankly.

I push the memory aside, opening my eyes, so I can confront his dark blue gaze. "Why are you here?" I demand furiously.

"Why weren't *you* in Nashville?"

The muscles in my neck twitch. I take in a noisy breath, so I won't tell him to go shove the neck of his guitar up his arrogant perfect ass. "I'm entitled to a vacation."

Wyatt lets out a dangerous chuckle. "Taken the exact moment we were supposed to see each other again? That shit won't work with me, Kylie. You should've known this would happen since you've been ignoring me ever since Thanksgiving."

Because he's using my full name and not Ky or Bluebird and since we once agreed to be honest with one another—even if that truthfulness aches like a fist to the heart—I give him the closest thing to a smile I can summon. "I'm entitled to a vacation that gets me away from you because seeing you always results in me losing my head for a few days." When a sensual grin begins to creep its way across his face, I immediately add, "And those few days always, *always* end with you letting me down for some reason or another and me wanting to knee you in the balls."

Grasping at his chest dramatically, he stumbles backward and winces. "You're scary when you're pissed, Wolfe." As I open my mouth to correct my last name—since I never changed it back to Wolfe following my divorce seven years ago—he presses his lips flat. "Don't even fucking think about it."

"Or you'll what? Spank me?"

Running his gaze suggestively up the length of my body, he says softly, deliberately, "That's coming anyway, Ky. You know how I feel about your ass."

Choosing to ignore that particular comment, I pull my hands out of my pockets, grab the cigarette tucked behind my ear, and slide it between my lips. Wyatt produces a lighter from his pocket and holds it six inches from my mouth. As I lean forward, I stare up at him from beneath my lashes.

"How'd you find me?" I demand. Taking a long inhale, I straighten my back and support my weight against the brick wall. "Well?"

"Disable the Foursquare, or I'll do it for you," he warns in that possessive voice that had me tripping all over myself a few years back. "Anyone can find you with that shit."

"Funny, thought I took you off my friends list."

"Didn't take Cal off it," he says, referring to one of his and my brother's bandmates.

"Nice." That single word sounds like poison rolling off my tongue. I take another drag of my cigarette, drop it to the black asphalt, and crush it beneath the heel of my boot. "Guess I see where Cal's loyalty lies. So, why'd you come?"

"Didn't want to think of anyone else's hands digging into that hair." He reaches out to me, sliding a few short strands through his fingertips. When I release a frustrated groan, he comes closer to me. "Couldn't stand the thought of you getting drunk and wrapping those legs around someone else."

"Why does it matter to you what I do in my downtime?" I breathe. "We're not exclusive, Wyatt."

"Maybe not, but it still won't stop me from wanting to keep you all to myself."

As if to prove his point, he squeezes my thigh, flicking the tip of his thumb back and forth across the V between my legs. My snug black jeans absolutely suck as a barrier. As heat speeds through my body, I bite my bottom lip and try to continue breathing like a normal person, so he's not aware of the effect he still has on me.

*Damn you, Wyatt.*

"Glad you have so much faith in me." This isn't the first time he's doubted me. I clear my throat to get rid of the dryness in the back of my mouth. "And now that you know my legs are safely locked at the knees?"

"I'm not leaving until you talk to me."

I narrow my chocolate brown eyes into thin slits. He swallows, making the tattoo across his throat appear as if it's moving. I don't need sunlight to know what it says. I was with him when he got it.

*All Does Not End Well.*

What's especially sad is that's exactly how things will go down if I go anywhere with Wyatt tonight or any other evening for that matter.

*So, why the hell do I still want him?*

"If I leave with you, you'll have no reason to find me through your friends anymore. I mean, isn't that your forte? A big jealous showdown followed by an even bigger letdown?"

The edges of his lips twitch up into an almost apologetic grin. "You forgot what happens between that showdown and letdown, Ky," he says.

I dig my nails into my palms, so I won't slap him. "Nah, I just didn't see a reason to mention *that*." And *that* would be the angry mind-fucking sex usually fueled by one of our more epic arguments.

Shoving my palms up against his muscular chest, I push myself away and walk around him. He grabs my wrist, the one with the nearly invisible scars racing across it, and spins me back around.

"Talk to me."

"You want me to talk? Well, here it is. I don't want you here. In fact, I'd rather be the third wheel to Heidi and the guy she just met," I say.

He shrugs off my words. *So much for talking.*

"You've got no fucking choice, beautiful."

"Of course I do."

But when I try to shake free of him again, he pushes my hands over my head, pausing when his gaze locks on my ring finger.

"Jesus, get that thing covered already," he snaps, his voice low but audible even over the sound of Cajun music pouring from the festival in the streets. "It's been seven years."

I skim the pad of my thumb over the tattoo of my ex's last name. "If you weren't here, you wouldn't have to look at it," I respond calmly despite the familiar harsh flash of pain in my rib cage. I want to choke this man. I want to curl my fingers around his freaking neck. I want to slap him and scream at him for all the times we've done this same thing.

After the storm is over—because I'm a glutton for punishment—I want him to kiss me. I want those feelings, the love, from Wyatt McCrae that I've been chasing for years. But that is the precise reason I'm here in the first place. I'm over chasing him. I've been over it since last year, and I have successfully stayed away from him.

*Until now.*

The tiny lines at the corners of his brilliant blue eyes tighten as he backs me up against the brick wall. The air leaves my lungs for all the wrong reasons.

"Do you really think I need to be with you to remember you let some fucker put his name on you?" He nudges my legs apart with his knee.

"You should've done it first."

"I'm doing it now."

"That would require a little more commitment than you telling me you want to take me back to your room and—"

But then Wyatt's mouth comes down on mine, shutting off my last few words. He lets go of my hands, and I drop them to his shoulders. I dig into his flesh because I don't want to let go. Because like so many times before, I'm so lost in him that it causes physical pain to every inch of my body.

I need to end this now.

I need to move on just like I planned.

"Wyatt," I start, but he rubs his thumb against the center of my lips and shakes his head.

"Just let go, Ky."

He replaces his thumb with his mouth, skimming his labret across my lips. The sensation of the metal makes me shiver, and I feel his slow smile. He thinks he's got me right where he wants me.

"I couldn't get you off my mind."

It must come as a shock to him when I pull back and put my index finger over his lips. "Glad you finally started to think about me after I left your bed." I zero my attention in on a piece of lint on my green T-shirt, taking my time to pick it off, so I can gather my thoughts. Finally, I look back up into his eyes. "But I'm still not fucking you tonight, babe."

# CHAPTER TWO

"You think that's what I came here for?"

Cocking my head a fraction so that my hair falls sideways over my face, I shove my hands deep into my back pockets. "Isn't sex what you always come to me for?"

He looks at me, *really* looks at me, and I can practically feel the heat from his disappointment seeping through my skin, burning its way through my body. That's the thing about Wyatt, about love in general. It always finds a way to get under my skin, scorching the hell out of me.

I glance away and squeeze my eyes shut, but he touches my chin gently, redirecting my face.

"If I only wanted someone to fuck, I would've just done it back in Nashville." A grin that somehow straddles the line between cocky and sheepish spreads across his face. Because I know precisely what he's going to say next, I flinch beforehand. "Instead, I declined."

*So, there was someone else.*

I tell myself to forget that thought because it's wrong. In order for there to be somebody else, Wyatt and I would have to be something to begin with.

I match his sarcastic grin with my own, and I pray it's just as infuriating. "Telling her you won't spend a second night with her isn't declining." When I laugh, there's a jagged edge to it. "I—"

"I didn't go through with it at all, beautiful. Believe it or not, I'm capable of not fucking everything with a pussy."

Silently, I tilt my head to one side and then the other, giving him a look of disbelief. He said nearly the same thing to me a year ago, a week before Your Toxic Sequel started their last tour. We weren't sleeping together at the time, and he sure as hell wasn't mine to lay claim to, but I desperately wanted to believe him.

Wyatt only lasted three days into the tour. I can't remember her name now—because there've been too many during our breaks and bullshit—but she was beautiful. And though I shouldn't have felt anything because I'd already expected the worse, it was impossible not to hurt when I saw her leaving his hotel room.

The tour was one of the last major blows, and the following Thanksgiving firmly secured what I already knew in my mind. *No matter how hard we try, there's no place for me whatsoever in Wyatt's life.*

I rub my right hand over my left shoulder. "I never said you screw everything with lady bits. Actually, I'm pretty sure you're damn selective. All I'm trying to—"

What I'm on the verge of saying is cut short by another couple wandering drunkenly into the alley. They're falling all over each other, laughing and groping. They don't seem to notice that we're here at all.

Shrugging away from Wyatt, I start in the direction of the club, and he follows right on my heels.

"At least they're having a good time," I say under my breath.

Of course, he hears me and snorts. "We'll have better once we're together again." He pauses, giving me time to counter or look up at him. When I do neither, he walks backward, speeding up so that he can face me. "But we won't be like them. I'm going to fuck you everywhere, Kylie, but not where anyone else will see it."

I'm at a loss for words, completely flustered, so I maneuver around him, keeping my gaze directed at the blur of people on the sidewalks. Our bodies brush, and he turns around to walk next to me. His fingertips find one of my belt loops, tugging me just a touch closer to him, but I still don't budge. Instead, I meet his stare. Wyatt's eyes—they're the reason we've been on this merry-go-round so many times. They carry all his emotions— the beautiful and hideous and heartbreaking.

"I'm exhausted," I say as the entrance to the warehouse nightclub comes into view. A long line is zigzagging around the club, and I realize there's no way we're getting back inside. I wrench my iPhone out of the pocket of my jeans to send Heidi a message to let her know what's going on, but she's already beaten me to it. I have two missed FaceTime calls and a text from just five minutes ago.

1:48 a.m.: *Saw you leave with HIM, so I came back to the room. Don't tell me Lucas ratted you out. You coming back after you're done? Finn might be stopping by later, so text me if you do.*

As I read, Wyatt stifles a noise that sounds suspiciously like laughter, and I cock my eyebrow. He's rocking back on his heels and working his thumbs together in front of him like a diabolical asshole.

"What?"

He shrugs his broad shoulders. "I know that look from anywhere. Somebody said something that pisses you off. And I bet you the panties you've got on that it's about me."

Pressing my lips together, I run the tip of my tongue along the roof of my mouth. Even my best friend assumes that when Wyatt McCrae shows up, the probability of me falling into bed with him as soon as he snaps his musical note–tattooed fingers is pretty damn high. "No, but I *am* sleepy as hell. So, we'll have to do this another time, and I'm going to respectfully keep my panties in place tonight."

"You sure know how to kick me in the balls, Ky, but I call bullshit." Ignoring my sharp intake of air, Wyatt runs his hand down my forearm. He doesn't stop until our palms touch, and he connects his fingers with mine. "I'll get us a taxi. We need to talk, and we're going to do it in my hotel room."

"I can get my own cab." When his grip on my hand tenses, I release a sigh. I can stand here all night and argue with him, but it's just going to make the situation worse. *Wyatt wants to talk? Fine. I can handle conversation.* "No trying to talk me into bed when we get to your room. And afterward, you'll let me enjoy the rest of my vacation?" I have only one more night left after this one, and damn it, I want to spend it in peace.

He nods almost convincingly, and a moment later, he flags down a taxi. I climb in and slide to the far left side of the car, and he comes in right after me, intensely gazing across the seat at me all the while. Judging by the hungry look in his eyes, I'd think I was sitting on the other side of a bed, naked and jutting out my B-cups while begging him for round two. Instead, I'm scowling in a cold, dark cab.

"Stop picturing me without my clothes."

Smirking, Wyatt lowers his mouth until it touches my cheek, and my shoulders lift up involuntarily. "Not naked, Ky, but fully clothed," he drawls softly enough so that only I can hear. "I'm thinking about how creative we'd have to be to fuck right here."

"What happened to the whole 'not where anyone else will see' spiel?"

"Emphasis on the word *creative*, beautiful."

I'm damn lucky that the cab driver chooses this second to clear his throat a few times, letting us know that he's waiting for a destination. The moment between us is ruined, and Wyatt and I break apart, glancing up to meet the man's gaze in the rearview mirror. "The Veranda," we say in unison.

As I lift my chin, he grins, and—*damn it*—my stomach and chest constrict. "You Foursquare stalked me down to the hotel?" I ask, my voice subdued but hard.

He shrugs a little too indifferently for my liking. "Better me than somebody else. I have good intentions."

*No, he has sweaty intentions.*

"It *was* someone else. It was Cal," I point out, rolling my eyes. When I catch the cab driver glancing up at us through the front mirror again, I lower my volume. "What time do you have to be back tomorrow to record?" The sooner Wyatt has to leave, the better, considering my heart and the short remainder of my vacation.

"There's not going to be any recording for a while."

"Y'all are finished already?" I can't keep the surprise out of my voice. The band just started to record. It's been a long time since Your Toxic Sequel made a new album without a lot of B.S. and delays.

"You're sexy as fuck when you say *y'all*. You know that, right?" He bites his lower lip and shakes his head from side to side.

Before I have a chance to smart off at him, he continues, "But no, we're not. Look, Lucas didn't want to mess up your trip, but Sinjin—"

The moment he says the drummer's name, I know nothing good will follow. "Oh shit," I murmur.

"We talked him into in-patient."

I bury my face in my hands. Other than Wyatt, Sinjin is my brother's oldest friend. Cal didn't join the band until six years ago after they had changed their name from Falling Anarchy to Your Toxic Sequel. In the fifteen years I've known Sinjin—fifteen years where he's become more like a brother to me than one of Lucas's friends—he's spent half of that time in and out of rehab.

"Was it bad?" I ask.

Even though Wyatt's mouth eases into a smile, I know this has to be painful for him. I always hate it when he's hurting because the crazy range of emotions that play out on his face makes everything from my throat to my belly feel like it's all tangled up in knots.

"Not as bad as last time."

My shoulders slump. The last time, Sinjin told me he wouldn't make it if he had to go away, and it scared the shit out of me. I start to tell Wyatt how relieved I am, but then I freeze. For some reason, he's suddenly more interested in his phone than talking about Sin or ogling, touching, or teasing me for that matter. He's holding something back.

"Okay, spill it, McCrae. What else happened?"

"He went off on Lucas's girl."

"Lucas's girl?" I repeat. "Please tell me you're not talking about Samantha." Lucas's ex-wife, Sam, has been an expensive pain in his ass since they were divorced years ago, and I pray she's not making trouble for him and the band again. That's the last thing YTS needs.

"I'm not going to beg you for information," I say through tightly clenched teeth, and the corners of Wyatt's blue eyes crinkle.

He's laughing at me. We're having a serious conversation, and this man is laughing at me.

*Unbelievable.*

"Yeah, Lucas's girl—damn near six feet tall with red hair. One minute, she's adjusting her halo, and the next, she's telling me to fuck off."

"Sienna," I say. She's the girl who's filling in for me as Lucas's assistant while I'm here.

Lucas had met her two years ago on a video shoot, but he'd screwed things up by kicking Sienna out of his house in the middle of a date, right after his ex-wife threatened to drop by. A week ago, when he discovered that the house he bought at an auction in Nashville—a house he doesn't honestly care for now—belonged to her grandmother, he moved in for the kill. He made her some fucked-up proposition, and he used me to help him. He used me to convince Sienna to work for him for ten days in exchange for the deed to her grandmother's home. I love my brother, don't get me wrong, but I despise him for exploiting her weaknesses to get what he wants.

"Okay…what exactly do you mean Sin went off on her? What did he say? Ugh, what did he *do*?"

Wyatt doesn't jump to answer me, so I bring up Sienna's name on my iPhone. Of course, it's much too late to call her, but it gets my point across.

"Kylie," Wyatt says. The taxi crawls to a stop just as he closes his large hand around my small one, stilling me. "I'll tell you upstairs." He keeps his blue eyes fastened on mine as he digs in his pocket to pay the fare.

"I can't stay long," I tell him a minute later as the driver pulls away. He touches the small of my back, leading me inside the hotel lobby, which is eerily quiet. "And I'll pay you my half of the cab fare when we get upstairs."

"No—to everything you said."

"Asshole."

He pretends he doesn't hear the insult as he pulls me into the elevator with him. He chooses the fifth floor, leans back against the wall, and lifts his eyes to the glass ceiling.

"I've got to say that I'm a little shocked you're not on the second floor. You know, since you tracked me all the way to this hotel. Guess I just figured you'd be on the same floor as me, too."

The elevator stops, and he lowers his chin so that we're face-to-face. "I can move rooms, Ky."

The door slides open to a few college boys who look stoned out of their minds. I step out first, barely missing the roving hands of the guy with the floppy hair. Wyatt comes out behind me, muttering a string of threats to the boy, and he grabs my waist to steer me in the right direction.

His suite is at the end of the hallway. As soon as we get to the door, he slides his hands into my back pockets and places his chin on the top of my head. We stay quiet for what seems like a long time as he breathes me in while I listen to the steady rhythm of his heart. The only other sound in the hall is a woman who creeps out of her room with an ice bucket, and she stops for a moment to give us a sleepy smile.

"What's this for?" I ask him.

"Because I told you I wouldn't try to fuck you if you came here," he says. Arching my body back, I look up at him and twist my lips to the side skeptically. "And because like I said earlier, I've fucking missed you since you left."

*But I didn't leave. You just weren't there when I needed you afterward, and I gave up.*

"I left because it wasn't going anywhere, because things are holding you back. The reason I didn't show this week is because I needed to…" I count backward from ten. "I've held on to you for so many years—through Brenna and the tours and all the other bullshit. I just need a chance to catch my breath."

Smiling sadly, he lets me go. As he turns to slide his room key into the card reader, I have to lean in close to him to hear his response. "You mean you needed a chance to fucking forget me."

*Yes.*

"No," I say.

"You're a bad, bad liar."

Despite my burning cheeks, I shiver when I step into his room. Whenever Wyatt stays in a hotel, as soon as he enters the room, he always adjusts the AC to its absolute lowest temperature, and this time is no different.

I sit on the end of the only bed in the room and play with the edge of the white cotton duvet. "So, tell me what happened with Sinjin and Sienna."

He sums it up quickly, explaining to me how Sin got so messed up that he not only talked shit to my temp, he threatened her, too. Since Lucas is hell-bent on possessing her, I have a feeling he was furious. By the time silence falls between Wyatt and me, my hands are balled into tight fists, leaving fingernail marks in my palms.

"And you're sure she's okay?" I finally ask.

Wyatt touches the side of my face. "I promise, okay? You can call her tomorrow. Stop trying to take care of everyone, and think about yourself this time."

I close my eyes. That's what he doesn't understand, what he doesn't want to acknowledge. I was thinking about myself when I came here. "I'm trying," I say in a strained voice. "I'm trying to do what's best for me."

"I'm not talking about what your head tells you is right."

"Don't tell me you're going to say to think with my heart."

"You said it. I didn't." He drops his hand from my face and lifts my fingers to his chest. "I need you around."

"I work for Lucas, so I'm around all the time."

He puts pressure on my hand, pressing it firmly against his chest, so I can feel how fast his heart is racing.

*God, why is he doing this to me? Why can't he just let us fall apart this time?*

"Fuck, then just give it one last time." Before I can speak, he moves both our hands to cup my cheek and then rests his forehead to mine. His naturally tan skin is hot to the touch. "I know why you came here of all places. You can lie to me all you want, Ky, but New Orleans is really where it started for us. Let's end it the right way. Spend the rest of your nights here with me, and when you go back to L.A...."

The last few words are broken off, leaving me to mentally fill them in for him.

*I won't fuck with you again.*

*You can finally forget me.*

*We can pretend like you never loved me.*

I wrap my fingers around his as if I need to hold on to him to stay upright. My chest is cold, and I try to figure out why. *Am I scared of what will happen if I spent tonight and tomorrow night with him? Or do I fear that he's agreeing to what I've already settled in my mind—to let things between us go after we're done here?* "And here I was thinking that you'd keep your word about not trying to get me into bed."

"Shit happens." When he grins, I smile back, but mine is shaky and unsure. "You in or not?" he demands.

Maybe it's because I still want Wyatt, and this might be the last time I can act on that desire before I move on. Or maybe it's because, not only a week ago, I convinced Sienna Jensen to take a chance on helping the man who screwed her over in the past. Either way, I know that I have to do this. I need to get this man out of my system.

"Yeah," I say. "I'm in."

Because Heidi soon texts me that she and Shiner Bock—or Finn as she calls him—are having "drinks" in our room, staying with Wyatt tonight becomes inevitable anyway unless I want to get another room.

To my surprise though, when he comes out of the shower with a towel slung low on his hips, he says, "Night, beautiful."

"You're going to bed?" I ask.

He stands on his side of the bed with his back turned to me but glances over his shoulder to cock an eyebrow. "Thought you were tired."

"Well, I am, but—" He drops the towel, revealing his incredible ass, and now, it's my turn to lift an eyebrow. "Really, Wyatt?"

He pulls on a pair of boxer briefs before turning around. Grinning, he jerks back the bedspread and stretches out on the oversized bed. *What the hell is he doing?*

"Come to bed."

I keep my eyes trained on him as I shimmy my jeans down, pull off my boots, and step out of them. I drag my T-shirt—which smells like booze, cigarettes, and my Betsey Johnson perfume—over my head and drop it beside my pants. "Got a shirt I can wear?"

His gaze dips to the tattoos on my shoulder and then to the big star in the center of my underwear. "Bag on the chair."

I grab the first thing I can find—a plain white T-shirt that smells like the Tide detergent his housekeeper washes his clothes in—and climb into bed with him as I finish pulling it on. When I move to lie down, he stops me, squeezing my hips gently between his hands.

"What?" I whisper breathlessly.

"How many of those things do you have now?" he asks, a serious expression on his face.

"What things?"

"Those goddamn blackbirds."

Unconsciously, my hand flies up to the left side of my chest to the tattoos, blackbirds in several different sizes. His T-shirt is covering most of them, but a few are still clearly visible. "Eighteen."

There's one for each time things have gone to hell between us and for every time I've screwed myself over. Even though they're not all because of him, my tattoos feel like eighteen tiny reminders of why accepting his challenge to stay with him for tonight and the next is as much of an omen as the ink itself.

*Seventeen too many tattoos.*

Wyatt inclines his head, and I almost expect him to say something else about the blackbirds, but when he speaks, it's about sex. *How typical.*

"I want nothing more than to wrap your legs around my shoulders and fuck you for the rest of the night." He pulls me on top of him, one leg at a time. "But in all the years we've been doing this, not once have I ever just slept with you. I figure if we're pulling the plug, we might as well do it just once."

The change of subject is like a fist to my stomach. It's so painful that it comes damn close to knocking the air out of my lungs. It's hard for me not to react, but I maintain my composure as I grip his shoulders tightly and lower my face down to his. Our lips graze.

"Sweet dreams." I don't give him time to respond. I roll off of him and curl up on my side with my back turned to his body.

We're quiet for several minutes before he makes a noise deep in his throat. "Come here, Ky."

His body finds mine in the dark, and he wraps his arm around my waist. He presses his lips against the tattoo between my shoulder blades—the caged bluebird. He picked it out for me a few years ago when I went with him to Atlanta for his father's funeral. It was supposed to symbolize happiness, a new beginning, but it hasn't done me much good.

"This, Kylie, *this* is how I need to remember you if you're done with me."

I curl my fingers around his hand, but I say nothing. I don't trust myself to speak.

It doesn't take long for him to fall asleep. He sleeps hard, sound, so he doesn't even flinch when I untangle myself from his body to turn back over to face him. I spend the next hour studying him, running my fingertips gently over his lips and the angles of his face. I etch every detail of him into my memory.

# CHAPTER THREE

"Fuck..."

The sound of Wyatt's voice cutting through the silence of the dark hotel room immediately snaps me out of my sleep, which is already fitful, thanks to him.

"Don't do that, Ky," he continues.

It takes a moment, which I spend with my eyes squeezed together, to realize that he's talking to me. And it takes another few seconds to grasp that at some point since I drifted off to sleep, he closed the tiny amount of space that had been left between our bodies earlier. He's wrapped his arm loosely around my waist and thrown one of his long legs across mine. And at some point, he got rid of his boxers so that I'd wake up to his very bare and—as much as I hate to admit it—incredibly epic hard dick against my stomach.

"Fuck is right," I mutter under my breath, echoing the word he used to wake me up.

"Kylie," he says my name again, this time in an urgent growl.

His hold on my waist tightens, and I flinch. I just know he'll mention how hot my skin feels, how he knows that every inch of my body is reacting to him right now.

But he doesn't say anything. And that's so untypical of Wyatt that I freeze. "Hmm?" When he doesn't rush to answer me, I drag open my eyes. "Wyatt, what the—" My words catch in the back of my throat.

*He's asleep.*

Wyatt is asleep, and he's saying my name desperately, hopelessly.

Call it cliché, but when the man I've loved since I lost my virginity to him at seventeen, the heavy sleeper that I'm just a few days away from leaving for good, calls out my name in his sleep, I've got no choice but to react.

*The question is: What am I supposed to do?*

Blowing a short blue strand of hair up and out of my eye, I curl my fingers around his shoulders. "You okay?" I nudge him back and forth.

He grinds his hips down and doesn't stop moving until we're crotch-to-crotch. My lips part slowly, and something that sounds like a rumble mixed with a moan comes out of my mouth. *What the hell is this man trying to do to me?*

"Wyatt, are you okay?" I repeat.

He exhales roughly. "I'm fine." He takes his hand away from my waist and moves it to my wrist, pulling my hand away from his shoulder. "I'm fine, but sleeping with you like this fucks me up." He grazes the tip of his tongue over my fingers and then sucks every other one completely into his mouth, skimming his straight teeth over the ridges of my knuckles.

Even though I know where this is going, I still gasp when he presses my palm to his erection. "Not fucking fair, McCrae," I say through a forced smile.

He closes my fingers one by one around his cock and guides my hand up and down his shaft. *No, this isn't fair at all.*

"Go back to sleep," I tell him.

He finally decides to open his eyes, parting them lazily so that he can stare at me unblinking. The back of my throat constricts, and inadvertently, I tighten my grip on him.

The side of his mouth with the labret pulls up into a wicked grin. "We've slept long enough, Kylie," he says. In a couple of well-executed swift motions, he pins me flat on my back and rolls over on top of me, his knees sinking into the mattress on each side of my hips. "Now, I'm planning to fuck you until my wake-up call."

When he tries to bend his head down to mine, I stop him, shoving my palm to his chest. I successfully succeed at *not* wandering my fingertips over the defined muscles taut beneath them, but the hand that's below his waist is not so resistant. It strokes him even harder. "And what time would that be?"

He moves his knee, and just when I think he's about to get off me, he nudges it between my closed thighs. I don't budge.

"Ten thirty," he says. "And your ass is mine 'til then."

Rolling my head to the side, I check the time on the digital MP3 clock sitting on the nightstand beside the hotel telephone. It's 5:53 a.m.

"Ambitious, aren't we, McCrae?" I ask, loving the way he shudders when I move my hand that's wrapped around him faster.

"One part ambition…" He reaches down and splays his hands on my thighs. He gives me a pointed look that clearly says he's not going to tell me part two until I oblige.

Sighing, I spread my feet apart, curling my toes in the crisp white sheets. "Now, part two?"

He caresses two fingers back and forth between my legs, sucking in a breath at how wet I've become, and he whispers something unintelligible about how much he hates my panties. It takes every ounce of self-control I have not to moan.

I want him to feel what I am feeling. I want him to experience every flash of exquisite torture and numbing pleasure. And I want him to feel it now. I move my hand up the length of him and then back down again, and I feel a thrill spread through my veins as a slow but uncertain smile builds on his face.

"That's my girl," he whispers into my ear.

"What's the other part?"

"Every time we see each other after this is all over and you're pretending like we don't mean shit to one another, I want to think back on how tonight and every night before it, your pussy belonged to me."

Without warning, he dips a finger into my panties and traces a heart around my clit. Wyatt's always hated playing his guitar with a pick, so his fingertips are rough. It's the most erotic, addictive thing I've ever felt—just a little painful but incredibly satisfying.

I'm not aware that I've let go of his cock, and I have started to dig my fingers into his back until a low noise slips from his lips.

"You trying to draw blood?"

I drop my hands. "Damn, sorry. You screw me up, too. You make me want—"

"What? Tell me what you want, beautiful."

*You make me want to keep trying.*

But even Wyatt's magic fingers, pierced lip, and dick aren't enough to make me want to go through all the emotional bullshit again. "You make me want to kick you in the throat for talking too much."

When he throws his head back and laughs, I kiss the tattoo on his throat.

"You are fucking amazing," he growls, pinning me back down.

He presses his mouth to his T-shirt that I'm wearing. My back arches as he skims his tongue around my breast, wetting the thin fabric. He pauses, his expression pensive for a few seconds, but then he makes up his mind. He shoves the tee up and over my head. Cupping my breast in his hand, he pulls my nipple into his mouth, sucking hard and using his teeth.

*God, he knows what that does to me.*

"You've always been amazing to me," he says in between strokes of his tongue.

His words push so many of my emotions to the surface at once that they all seem to crash into each other, causing my head to spin and my vision to cloud. What I feel is love, but there's something else, too—something that's bitter and nauseating but not quite hatred. And I realize that I need to say so much to him before we're done. There's so much I hadn't even considered when I came here to get away from him.

But putting everything out there will have to wait.

Because if Wyatt's going to look at me a few months from now and think about what we did in our final hours, I want him to remember how I rocked his world, not how I turned into a sentimental sap.

I curve my fingers back around his erection. Racing my free hand up his chest, I bring my face up to his. When I clench the skin close to his neck, he groans and squeezes my clit between his thumb and forefinger.

"Fuck me," I pant.

He leans over and rummages around in the nightstand drawer. "Shit," he says in a harsh whisper. When his eyes meet mine again, his gorgeous features are worked into a frown. He rubs his palm back and forth over the top of his head, mussing his short blond hair. "Ah hell, I've cockblocked myself."

Because my head is obviously not in the right place, I release an exasperated moan. "Well, stop."

He makes a soft noise that sounds like a chuckle against the column of my throat. "Trust me, it was unintentional." He rubs my center faster, and my legs tremble. "Damn, I need you."

My hand finally closes around his neck, not hard but just enough for him to growl a curse against my mouth. "Why not now?" I demand as he pulls himself out of my grip.

He glances up at me for a moment. "Because as good as I know how you'll feel, I'm not prepared."

Realization dawns on me that he's condomless. I nod my head in understanding even though for the life of me, I can't understand why a rock star would leave the house without one. Before he even has the chance to think about asking me if I'm willing to go without, I shake my head.

He crawls down the length of my body and kisses the insides of my thighs. "We'll just do this the hard way."

My muscles grow tense as he sucks hungrily on my clit. My next question is muffled because I cover my mouth with my wrist to keep from crying out. Once I catch my breath, I tease, "Wake-up call, my ass."

"Don't worry. Tonight, your ass and that wake-up call are mine."

*What exactly does he call this then?* He lowers his mouth to my sex again, and I bite down on my tongue as if it'll keep me from making a sound, but finally, I whimper.

Because Wyatt knows me so well, he leans away from me for a split second. "Oh, you're mine right now, Kylie. It only takes a little improvisation."

"Improvisation?" I repeat.

He nods, his dark blond hair tickling my thighs. "Like this." With one hand gripping my waist, he parts my wet slit with the other, and without warning, he pushes two fingers inside me. I ball my hands into fists, clutching onto the crumpled cotton sheets.

"And this." The tip of his tongue races around my clit as his fingers glide back and forth inside me.

His rhythm makes me dizzy. I buck my hips toward him. He releases a low sound that seems to hum through my body. Wyatt and I have done this more than once. We've fucked so many times that I've lost count, but this is the first time that I've felt like I'll catch fire.

Keeping his fingers deep inside me, the pad of his thumb replaces his tongue as he strategically kisses up my body. With one kiss on each hipbone, I shiver. After a kiss on my belly button, he pauses to circle it with his tongue, and when I try to grasp his hair, he catches my wrist. And then he kisses each of my breasts, using everything from his teeth to his piercing to get a rise out of me. By the time our bodies are flush with each other again, I'm a wreck.

"More improvisation?" I moan.

He hooks his free hand under my knee and wraps my leg around his waist. I follow suit with my other leg, clenching him tight.

"Mmhmm, like this." His mouth covers mine, nibbling my lips and battling my tongue.

So, when I come intensely a moment later, whispering that I love him, my words are nothing more than muffled sobs.

\*\*\*

Wyatt is in the shower when the alarm on my phone suddenly goes off at exactly six twenty a.m. At first, I don't do anything to silence it. One, my legs are still shaky from his *improvisation*. Two, my phone is all the way across the room, lodged down in the back pocket of my jeans. And three, I love The Black Keys, and I could probably listen to my "Lonely Boy" ringtone over and over again for the rest of the morning. But when the person staying in the next room over taps gently on the wall, I suck it up and slide out of bed. As I steady myself and tiptoe over to my pants, I try not to think about why our neighbor didn't knock on the wall five minutes ago.

I bring my jeans back over to the bed, pluck my iPhone out of them, and drop them on the floor. As I deactivate the alarm, I pause, my gaze zeroing in on the reason for the reminder: *CHECK ON LUCAS'S ATL FLIGHT!*

Last night, just as Heidi and I were leaving our hotel room, I realized that I had never confirmed today's flight with Sienna. It was too late to call her then, so I had tipsily left a message for myself. It was a stupid move on my part because I should have taken care of it immediately.

"I go on vacation, and I'm still doing work." As I climb back into Wyatt's bed, I know I shouldn't complain. Making sure my brother's trip to Atlanta goes smoothly is my responsibility, it's what he pays me for, and it's something I shouldn't have left on a to-do list for my replacement just because I was in a hurry to get the hell away from Wyatt.

I log in to both of Lucas's email accounts and search through the last six days of messages three times, going back to well before I left for vacation. Finally, I give up and send Sienna a text message.

6:32 a.m.: *Hey, babe, what email address did you send Luke's confirmation for the flight to Atlanta to? Don't see it in the regular email and was worried.*

A few more texts and a thirteen-minute phone call (where I fib and tell her I'm just checking up on her because I had a bad dream that today's flight went horribly) later, I'm frantically scouring every travel website in existence for a couple of tickets.

"You're sexy when you make that face," Wyatt says, flipping over on his side. He's been lying beside me since a few minutes into my conversation with Sienna, but this is the first time he's faced me directly since getting out of the shower. He traces his fingers in lazy circles across my kneecap, finally pressing the end of his thumb and middle finger against the sensitive spots that make my muscles jump.

He did the same thing and more the entire time I was on the phone with Sienna, driving me to distraction.

"Concentration is—" I start, but he cuts me off.

"If you pull a fucking Lucas and say it's my friend, I swear I'll lay you down right here and show you how easy it is to forget about being an assistant."

"No protection, babe. Remember?" *I refuse to go down that road with him.*

He snorts. "Ky?"

I glance up from Travelocity.com and the roaming gnome's creepy face to raise an eyebrow.

"My tongue doesn't need a condom."

Remembering precisely where his tongue had been before I started frantically searching for plane tickets makes my mouth go dry. "Don't you have a song to write, or…I don't know, a guitar to strum while I do this?"

"Guitar is in there." He jerks his thumb toward the hotel closet. Laying his head on my lap, he blows on my belly button. "Besides, I'm resting. Cal and I are road-tripping it, starting tomorrow."

I clench my phone but manage to keep my brown eyes focused on the screen. *So, he's really leaving tomorrow morning.* "Really? What for?"

"Last minute guest thing for another band."

Now, he's got my full attention. The search for my brother's flight is momentarily forgotten as I place my phone down beside me and frown. "A guest gig? That's not really your type of thing, Wyatt. Is everything alright?" When he nods, I narrow my dark eyes suspiciously. "Are they paying you in booze and vag?"

"God, you're so eloquent sometimes." He reaches up to my face and tucks a strand of hair behind my ear. He moves his hand, and when I readjust the same lock of hair, putting it back where it was, he flashes his teeth at me. "No, it's for Cal's cousin. They're transitioning members and had some prior commitments. It's only a few shows."

This is not the Wyatt McCrae I know. *My* Wyatt would tell Cal's cousin to go fuck himself.

"Is everything alright with YTS? You and Lucas aren't ending your bromance, are you?" My tone is playful yet slightly serious.

The corner of his lip tugs up just a bit. "Everything's fine."

I tighten my shoulders, so I won't drop them in relief. Your Toxic Sequel is like my family, and I'd take their breakup as badly as

I would my own parents. I pick up my phone, but I can't resist peeking over the edge of it to study him. "You and Cal are doing bar shows?"

"Yeah." He must not miss how my features suddenly go taut. He curls his long fingers around my hand and brings it down to rest on his chest. "What's that look for?"

"Can't find a flight," I say sharply.

"You don't want me to do bar shows." He's using *the voice*, the one that's an octave higher than how he usually speaks. It's tender and laced with a healthy dose of surprise.

"Babe, you can do whatever you want." Using the hand he's not holding, I jab at the keypad on my phone. "I just want to find Lucas—" But Wyatt stops me mid-sentence by plucking my phone out of my grasp. "What are you doing?" I ask in a heated voice.

Sitting up, he punches a number in before tossing the iPhone into my lap. "Helping you work out Lucas's bullshit again." His incredible blue eyes are full of amusement as he rolls over to the other side of the mattress.

For a long time, I stare at his chest, specifically at the tattoo on his rib that says, *Worse At What I Do Best*, before I climb out of bed.

When I turn my back to him and drop my gaze to my phone and the number Wyatt has saved as *Private Jet*, he adds, "How the hell do you think I got here from Nashville so fast last night?"

*Oh hell.* He didn't mention he had gone through so much trouble to get to me. I assumed he flew in through Southwest, his favorite airline. I'm glad that my face is turned away from him, so he can't see my look of surprise and then how I have to squeeze my eyes shut because of the sudden burn I feel from the tears threatening to escape.

"Thanks for this." I pick up and drag my green shirt from last night over my head. "For the travel information, I mean." My jeans go on next, and when I wiggle my bottom to finish pulling them up, he sighs.

"Hate to see that ass disappear." Because my bra cups aren't exactly overflowing, Wyatt's always had a thing for my butt. "It's too fucking perfect to cover up, beautiful."

I flush. "I'll see you around."

He doesn't respond until I've opened the door to his hotel room, and what he does say will stay with me for the rest of the day. "Tonight, Kylie. Tonight you're fucking mine."

*As if I need a reminder.*

My face is still prickly when I let myself into my room five minutes later. Cautiously, I peek around the corner to where our queen-size beds are separated by only a nightstand, and I see that Heidi is alone. She's sitting on her bed in a midriff-baring tee and boy shorts, plucking food off a tray loaded with the continental breakfast.

"You're up early," I say.

She takes a long sip of coffee and makes a face at the Styrofoam cup. "So are you. Did you screw Prince Albert to get him out of your system?" When I slide down on the edge of my bed to face her, she lets out a dramatic sigh. "You didn't, did you?"

Heidi's been my friend for the last four years. I met her on tour when she was dating the lead singer of the band that opened for Your Toxic Sequel. We bonded instantly over our mutual love of music. Our similar backgrounds—my parents are youth ministers, and her dad is a former televangelist—brought us even closer. She's been there for me through the bullshit and the tears and our inability to commit because of the past, and she *gets* me

When I glance up at her, I don't even try to keep the misery from creeping its way onto my face. "He took the Prince Albert out a couple of years back, remember?"

I still have memories of the tiny piercing that was on the head of Wyatt's cock, and they're all vivid enough to flood my mouth with moisture.

She snorts and bites into her bagel. "Sorry, I don't keep up with what Wyatt McCrae is doing with and to his junk."

"Which is why we're friends." I scan through my phone, searching for the number Wyatt programmed earlier. "Sin is back in rehab," I say quietly. She's going to find out sooner or later, and it's better if I tell her myself.

She sinks her small teeth into her lip. Heidi's been around for a lot of Sinjin's ups and downs, too. "What the fuck?" she finally demands.

So, I tell her everything Wyatt told me last night, and when I'm done, she shakes her head to each side. "What's going to happen to him?"

"I don't know, but as soon as I speak to Lucas directly, I'll sure as hell find out." In the meantime, I need to handle his flight details before I can even think about confronting him. I fish out my credit cards from the nightstand drawer.

Heidi cocks an eyebrow as I take off in the direction of the bathroom. "If you want to talk dirty, I can cut you a discount," she calls after me.

I spin around to face her. "It's impossible for me to take you seriously when you've got cream cheese on your upper lip," I say.

She wipes it off with the back of her hand, smearing it even more.

"Making a call for Lucas before I talk to him about Sin. Be out in a little." I start to close the bathroom door, but then I poke my head out. "How was Shiner Bock?"

Heidi looks confused for a moment, but then she figures out to whom I'm referring to and laughs. "Eh . . . I guess he was okay." She lifts her hand, wobbling it from side to side. "Finn and I are having drinks tonight. You should come."

*Meaning he has a friend.* I roll my eyes. "So-so isn't exactly grounds for drinks and round two, babe, but I'll think about it," I say as I close the restroom door and dial the number Wyatt gave me.

Arranging the flight for Lucas takes longer than I initially assumed. By the time I'm done and I've emailed the details to Sienna, assuring her that Lucas will be okay with the extravagant cost, Heidi is passed out in bed, making soft noises that she always swears isn't snoring.

I curl up in my bed and grab my iPod and earbuds from under my pillow. Out of habit, I let the sound of Chevelle rock me to sleep.

# CHAPTER FOUR

"So, how do you and Heidi know each other?" Finn asks me after he takes a swig of his drink-of-choice for the evening, Bud Light.

We've been out barhopping for at least an hour, and this is the first thing he's actually said to me all night. All he's talked about is the gym, and although Heidi claims he's from Florida, I expect him to bring up tanning and laundry at any moment.

"You two work together?" he continues before I can answer his first question.

Across the table, Heidi's cornflower blue eyes widen slightly. She gives a slight jerk of her head that Shiner Bock and his friend, James, don't seem to notice.

I down a sip of my drink before asking him, "Hmm?"

Shiner Bock curls his arm around Heidi's bare shoulders and shifts a lock of her wavy brown hair through his fingers. "Customer service rep, right?"

*So, that's what Heidi's calling phone sex now.* Smoothing my hair back, I shake my head, and Heidi's nervous smile—the one that, paired with her bright red lipstick and the lighting in the bar, makes her look like a hot version of The Joker—stretches across her face. "No, I'm my older brother's personal assistant."

Heidi instantly relaxes and bobs her head up and down in agreement. If she felt the need to lie about what she does for a living—and she's damn proud about her voice-banging gig—then things must have gone much better with Shiner Bock than she let on this morning.

"You like it?" he asks.

I squint down at my drink. "Best job in the world." *Besides the fact that I'm almost always with the band.* That's one of the reasons Wyatt and I have never been able to move forward properly. I know what goes on behind the scenes. There's always been too much temptation, and after Brenna, too much doubt on my end about what's happening when I'm not around. And then, there's the fact that I've had to watch Sin's fast, tumultuous downfall over the last few years.

Yes, I love my job, and I love Your Toxic Sequel, but sometimes it's too much, even for me.

A hand brushes up against my thigh. I flinch and turn my head a fraction to James, who's smiling back at me. He's good-looking enough. He has a dark tan, like Shiner Bock, with auburn hair and sea green eyes. Unlike Shiner Bock, he's taller, standing at least a half a foot over my five-four stature. And he's got a bad case of *the feels*. This is the fourth time in the last hour when James's fingers have made contact with my body, which includes two "accidental" boob pokes and one bold-as-hell ass grope.

"You okay, Kyla?" he asks.

"I'm good." I ignore the fact that he doesn't know a little detail like my name.

His hand inches down toward my knee, causing me to let out a little breath of relief. "I was just asking what your brother does."

"He's in a band," Heidi and I say at practically the same time. After running my tongue down over the center of my upper lip, I continue, "My brother is in a band, and I travel around with them." Lifting my beer to my mouth, I drink a quarter of the contents in one gulp.

James's eyes narrow skeptically. "Anyone worth listening to? Or one of those small town things?"

The derision in his voice snaps my head up. Setting my drink down on the table a little too hard, I give him a withering glare.

"Actually, I've found that some of my favorite bands are the ones who are small town things." *Douche bag.* I'm already on edge because Wyatt hasn't texted me, and Lucas brushed me off earlier this afternoon when I called to ask him about Sinjin, so I inhale and exhale a couple of times before I speak. "But, yeah, I think Lucas's band is worth listening to. My brother fronts Your Toxic Sequel."

Beneath the muted lights hanging overhead, James flushes—three different shades of red, in fact. When he moves his hand away from my knee, I scoot my chair as far away from him as the limited amount of space will allow. Across the table, Heidi glances down at her napkin, and Shiner Bock chokes on his drink and then pounds on his chest a few times.

"You're kidding, right?" James asks.

As I move my head from side to side, he gives Heidi and his friend a look before turning his eyes back to me.

Heidi clears her throat. "She's not."

Because James and Shiner Bock more than likely think I'm the biggest bitch who ever existed, the next twenty minutes of conversation is a strained and incredibly awkward tribute to my brother's band. Finally, James wanders off because he swears he sees one of their other friends.

Heidi shoots me a sympathetic look and mouths, *Sorry.* I respond by giving her an apologetic smile. It's not her fault that I'm in a bad mood. The last thing I want to do is ruin her final evening in New Orleans by being a buzzkill.

When I push my chair back, she bites the corner of her bottom lip, frowning, as she starts to get up too, but I shake my head. "I've got to take care of a few things in the room, but I'll be back." Of course, I have no intention of returning, and I'm sure she already realizes that.

"Text me if you need me, okay?" she says, which actually means, *Come drink with us if Wyatt lets you down again.*

"I will." I force a smile as I pluck my thin skull-print jacket off the back of the chair and slide it on over my black lace halter top. "Nice to meet you, Shi...*Finn.* Tell James I had fun." *Wherever the hell he is.*

As I leave the building, I'm able to tell James good-bye myself. He's at the bar, leaning over a shot glass and making conversation with a skinny girl who has purple-and-green spray-in color blended into her blonde hair. My eyes connect with his, and he smiles sheepishly. I raise my hand to wave, and he lifts up his chin in return.

"Better you grope her ass than mine," I grumble.

Stepping out onto Canal Street in the French Quarter to walk back to my hotel, I pull my jacket tightly around me. It's unusually cold tonight, and I wish I would have brought along my coat instead. I walk faster as I dodge the crowd, hoping that I'll warm myself quickly.

Though I really want to, I fight the urge to stop and check my phone to see if Wyatt called. I know he hasn't, and looking at a screen that shows nothing but the background image of me with Cal and Sinjin making duck faces and holding up metal horns in a bathroom will just turn me into a frustrated pile of whiny-ass. Plus, it's cold as hell, and I want to get back to my hotel room sooner rather than later.

My head is down, and I'm contemplating a long bath as I dip into the front entrance of The Veranda ten minutes later. I'm not aware that someone has been calling my name until that person grabs my wrist as I skulk through the middle of the lobby.

"You're fucking deaf, Wolfe," a male voice says from behind me.

I spin around so fast that my pumps make a squeaking noise on the glossy floor. I pause for a moment, taking in Cal's lanky but toned body and disheveled shoulder-length jet-black hair, before I launch myself into his arms. He's initially surprised, but then he wraps me up in his arms as I bury my face into the front of his shirt.

"You do realize that I could've maced you, right?" I demand. "What the hell are you doing here?"

He pulls away from me, smirking, his dark eyes amused. "Flew in, so I can head out with McCrae tomorrow morning."

Somehow, sleep and making sure my brother made it to Atlanta in one piece completely shoved that little detail out of my head. *Wyatt and Cal are going on the road together…to play bar shows.* "I'm sure that'll be fun."

Cal winks at me. "Fuck yeah, it will. Shitty food and grimy hotel rooms." We both know that he and Wyatt are more than capable of paying for any hotel they want while they're on the road, so it's my turn to look skeptical. "And before I forget and you blast me, sorry about the Foursquare thing."

"Yeah, about that…" I pull away from him and nod my head toward the elevators. He follows alongside me. "I'd actually forgotten, but thanks for reminding me that I need to kick your ass."

"I had to tell him, Kylie. He loves—"

"Don't," I say, my voice suddenly deep and all sorts of screwed up. "Please don't, okay?" I don't need Cal telling me how much Wyatt loves me because it will only be an assumption.

Wyatt has not once actually said the words to me himself. The closest he's ever come was almost four years ago after our millionth break from each other. We lasted approximately five weeks without having any contact. Finally, he showed up at my parents' house in Atlanta while we were celebrating Lucas's twenty-fifth birthday. Wyatt and I sat outside, alone together, on the front porch swing with a foot of space between us.

"I fucked up, huh?" he asks me, referring to the cause of our latest fallout.

This time, he confronted me again about cutting, something I haven't done in years, and it wouldn't have been so bad if he gave me a chance to speak during his rant. But he simply went on and on, reminding me of my ex, until the only thing I wanted was to get away from him and the pressure. So, rather than try to defend myself, I did just that.

I ran like a coward.

I ran like I would never have to face him again.

I take a deep breath, focusing my gaze on the bright orange and yellow tulips in my mom's garden. "Yeah, you did. You screwed up, and I want to hate you for it, but I can't." I tremble violently while I sink my nails into my palms, hoping to control myself enough to finish speaking to him. "Just because I wear long sleeves or refuse to show you my wrists doesn't mean I'm cutting, Wyatt. Because I'm not. I'm not saying that I don't have moments when I feel like the world is crashing down on me, that I'm nothing but—"

*As the words catch painfully in the back of my throat, he reaches out, raveling his long fingers in the hair at the nape of my neck.*

*"You're everything. At least to me. You always have been, and that's why I said what I did. I never want you to hurt, you got me, Kylie?"*

*His blue eyes are hard and honest, stripping me down to my soul, and I nod. He dips his gaze down to my shoulder, and since I know what's coming next, I answer before he has a chance to ask.*

*"Twelve." But I don't tell him that the newest one is there because of me. I let myself down by being a coward and refusing to face him.*

*"Fuck," he says between clenched teeth. "I'm sorry, Ky. I'm so goddamn sorry."*

"I'm sorry Kylie." Cal's voice reaches into the vivid memory, dragging me away from it. "I hate to see you hurting," he adds.

I nod stiffly. "It's fine."

Cal stops with me at the elevator door. He doesn't come inside, but he gives my hand a tiny pump as I shuffle in. "I'm going to grab something to eat before the fucker comes back with the rental car. You coming?"

*So, that's where Wyatt went instead of keeping his word to me—to pick up a rental car, so he can go play a few shows with a band he doesn't even know.* God, I know I shouldn't be bothered over learning that, but I am. I can't help it. Stepping aside so that an over-glitzed woman on wobbly heels can come into the elevator, I shake my head, my movements stiff. "I've got to do laundry before Heidi and I pack up to go back to L.A., tomorrow night."

Cal snorts. "You're officially the lamest person I know."

As the doors close, I flip him off. Laughing, he shakes his head and returns the gesture.

"Should've gone with him," Glitzy says. She's balancing herself in the corner, squeezing her knees together like she has to pee. Releasing a massive hiccup, she adds, "He was hot and looks like that guy from that one band." She bites her lip and scrunches her face, seemingly trying to remember the name of the band.

Thankfully, the elevator shudders to a stop on the second floor before she can venture a guess.

"Thanks for the advice," I say as I speed walk off into the hallway.

My room is an inferno when I step inside. My plan to sink myself into a scalding bath flies out the window, so I throw my license and credit cards inside the nightstand drawer and grab my iPod from its spot under my pillow. I drop my change purse inside my laundry bag and leave the room, and this time, I take the stairs to the dungeon-like basement where the laundry room is located.

I'm the only person in the laundry room, and it's probably because everyone else in this city had the good sense to go out tonight. I slide in my earbuds, turn on a random playlist, and since I have access to all the machines, I sort my clothes into three piles— whites, darks, and my delicates—instead of the two loads I planned on.

While the washer runs, I wait patiently without looking at my phone, but as I load the dryers, I can't help but finally check. *Still nothing from Wyatt or Lucas.* I have too much pride to contact Wyatt, so my brother is the lucky recipient of my text message.

12:43 a.m.: *Call me about Sin tomorrow, okay? Love you, Lucas.*

Since it's 1:43 in Atlanta right now, I don't expect him to reply. I lay my phone facedown on one of the machines and crank the volume on my iPod even higher. As I insert quarters into the gleaming white Whirlpool dryers, I can't resist singing along to Weezer. "...my love is a life taker."

The next line of "Say It Ain't So" is cut off because I notice a new scent in the small laundry room. It's clean and masculine, and as I breathe it in, the only image that comes to mind is the top of Wyatt's head visible between my legs.

"I didn't Foursquare where I was this time," I say softly.

When Wyatt presses his tall body up against my backside, my muscles weaken. He gently removes my earbuds, and his lip ring teases my skin as he growls into my ear, "I've never seen someone's hips move like that to *that* song." He's always disliked *that* song because the lyrics are about addiction and heartbreak, and they hit a little too close to home, reminding him of his parents. He doesn't mention this though as he places my iPod beside my phone. He brushes his fingertips down my chest, skimming over my breasts, until they finally stop at the closure on my jeans. "And no, you didn't have to Foursquare yourself this time."

*No, I guess not when we have a mutual friend who's bound and determined to see us together. Cal and I are going to have a serious heart-to-heart about his inability to keep his mouth shut.*

"Did you get your car?" I breathe, turning to face him.

He nods and returns his hands to the button on my pants. I step backward, and he follows until I bump into the dryer.

"And I've got a pocket full of…"

His voice trails off as I run my palms over his back pockets, and foil crunches in the left one.

"I thought you forgot about me," I admit.

He crushes my body to his and shakes his head. "Never, Kylie."

I reach up and touch the sides of his face, threading my fingers into his wheat-colored hair.

"And besides, I called and messaged you many, many times."

My lips quirk up skeptically. I ease away from him and flip over my phone to see if I have any missed calls. There are none from Wyatt. "Did you dial the wrong number?"

"Unless the wrong number has your voice on the answering machine, beautiful." He plucks his phone from his back pocket and scrolls through a list of names. When he reaches mine, he recites the number. "That's right, isn't it?"

"That's my home number, babe. I use it, like, once a year." I pull his phone from his grip and examine the entry he's made for me. A soft, almost nervous laugh bubbles from the back of my throat as I realize he has my numbers saved backwards—my cell phone is listed as my home number and vice versa. As I correct both numbers, letting him know about the mix-up in the process, the irritation I've felt the majority of the night drifts away.

*Wyatt kept his word, and he came down here to find me.*

*He sought me out for our last night together.*

Realizing this sends both pleasure and pain throbbing through my chest. My body threatens to crumble, but I hold on to the dryer behind me for support.

"I can be upstairs in fifteen minutes, and then we can…" I stop speaking for a moment, my eyebrows pulling together, as he leans far over to lock the laundry room door. "What are you doing?"

I gasp when he jerks me to him, finally undoing the pesky top button of my jeans with his other hand at the same time. In one rough motion, he drags the denim along with my panties down my hips.

*Oh. My. God.*

His hands spread across my ass frantically, and the initial slap he gives my backside sends a delicious sting across my skin. Bending his head slightly, he plunges his tongue into my mouth. I kiss him back just as greedily, meeting the slightest movement of his mouth with my own. As I taste Guinness on him, I remember the night of my twenty-first birthday when we downed too many Black Velvet drinks at the Halloween Rock Ball where YTS was playing. We'd had sex, hard and frantic, in the dressing room's bathroom before they went back on stage to play.

"You taste so good," I murmur.

As he glides his finger between my legs, a look of satisfaction takes over his face. I fumble with the button on his jeans just as he flicks his tongue across his fingertip, savoring my flavor.

"Not as good as you taste," he growls. "Bend over, Ky."

He doesn't wait for me to comply. He simply turns me around, so I'm facing the dryer. I grasp the sides and lean over it, shuddering at how the warmth from the machine spreads through my chest, at how the vibration sends more heat spiraling to the pit of my stomach.

Wyatt draws away from me only for a moment, but when he returns, I feel him, hard and long, against my bare ass. "You know this isn't it for us tonight," he says, cupping my sex.

When I mutter, "It better not be," he chuckles into my ear and glides his cock between my slick folds. He slides himself against me, back and forth, testing my wetness, before thrusting into me.

A sigh escapes my lips, and I grip the corners of the dryer tighter. I rock my hips back and forth, meeting his deep thrusts. He presses his lips to my bluebird tattoo and groans.

"Fuck, Kylie."

Reaching around me, he squeezes my clit softly, and I gasp.

"Don't stop. God, don't stop."

Because I need this from him. I need everything he can give me tonight, so I can move on and not want more.

"Harder?" He rubs my center in quick circular motions.

Strands of my dark hair cling to my damp forehead as I nod. "Please."

With his free hand, he clutches my hip and slams into me. I just know that I am going to scream. I'm going to scream, and the hotel staff will rush down here to find us screwing like rabbits over their brand new Whirlpool dryer. Then, I'll be banned from The Veranda for life.

For this, it's worth it.

As the moan builds in my throat, he lets go of my hip and slides his finger into my mouth. When I bite down on it, hard, he releases a low noise.

"Come for me, Ky."

I shake my head. "Not yet, not until—"

"Come for me," he repeats. "You've got me all night. You've got me for as long as you want. I want to hear you come."

I'm still moving my head furiously from side to side even as the orgasm rips through me. I tighten up around him, clenching his cock inside me, until a moment later when he trembles. We don't make a sound or a movement for what seems like hours.

At last, I feel his lips part between my shoulder blades. It takes a second, but I finally make out what he's saying.

"That's my fucking girl."

Breathing heavily, I turn around, so we're face-to-face. He touches his lips to my forehead, then to my lips, and finally, to the tip of my nose. "Thanks," I murmur. I place my palms flat against his chest, not to push him away, but so I can feel the unsteady drumming of his heart. "I mean it. Thanks."

Keeping his blue eyes on my face, he slips my jeans back up and grins when I shift uncomfortably. "I meant what I said, Kylie. You've got me for the rest of the night. I don't want there to be any—" He's cut off by the doorknob jiggling.

I mutter a curse and scramble to button my pants and adjust my halter top as he pulls up his jeans.

"Kylie?" Heidi's muffled voice filters in from the other side of the door. "Please tell me you're in there. I lost my key to the room, and it's booked under your name, so they won't give me a replacement."

Relieved, I sag against Wyatt's chest, and he strokes his hand down my spine. This slight motion brings me close to unraveling, even closer to spinning out of control. Gripping a handful of his t-shirt, I clear my throat before answering Heidi. "Yeah, let me grab my stuff. I'll be upstairs in a few, okay?"

"Why's the door locked?"

Wyatt grins, but I place my finger over his mouth and give him a warning glare. He retaliates by squeezing my breast.

"It locks when it shuts. I've got an armful of laundry, so I'll be up there in five, okay?"

She mumbles something inaudible and then calls out, "Whatever, see you in a few."

I count to a hundred before I yell out her name. When she doesn't answer, I look up into Wyatt's eyes. "You like to make your presence known, don't you?" My voice is teasing, but the look on his face is serious. The pit of my stomach coils. I don't want seriousness from him—not tonight.

"Where you're concerned, Ky, yeah, I do."

I touch the base of my throat, massaging the area carefully, and watch him as he heads to the door. "You'll be in your room?"

He glances over his shoulder. "I'll be there."

"Cal's not going to show up, is he?" I ask as he steps out into the hallway.

Wyatt scratches a hand through his blond hair and cocks his head to the side, grinning. "Not if he doesn't want his fucking fingers broken."

"Well aren't you Mr. Effing Possessive."

As he closes the laundry room door, he rakes his deep blue eyes over me, sending another flash of desire speeding through my body. "Damn right I am, beautiful."

Finally alone, I smile to myself as I stuff my laundry, which is still slightly wet, into the bag before I take the elevator back to my room. Heidi's standing outside of our door with her arms crossed over her chest, scowling.

I stop in my tracks. "You okay?"

"Finn bailed on me, but I'm alright." She stretches her arms out over her head and yawns theatrically. "I just want my bed." As I dig in my back pocket for the key card, she tilts her head to the side. "You look way too happy for having just done laundry."

I bite my lip to suppress a grin as I unlock our door. I'm contemplating whether or not I should tell her, but then I flip on the light switch.

And my heart sinks.

Every inch of our room has been rummaged through. There are clothes, both Heidi's and mine, thrown all over the place, and all the dresser drawers have been pulled out.

"What are you—" Heidi begins, sliding past me to get inside. Like me, she stops in her tracks. She sums up exactly how I'm suddenly feeling in the single word she says next. "Shit."

# CHAPTER FIVE

Over the last several years, I've gotten used to dealing with cops, not because of myself but due to the notoriety of the band. There's the loud and completely out of hand hotel parties, Sin's drunken habit of dropping his pants and pissing on the side of the street (or wherever else he happens to be standing at the time), and of course, my brother's foul temper, which has gotten Lucas into trouble time and time again. Still, I've got to admit that going through the motions of filing a report with the police officer who shows up at this hotel drains my energy.

Since we can't go back into our room yet, the staff at The Veranda is nice enough to set us up in one of the smaller event rooms located on the main floor while they prepare us another room. A Happy Anniversary sign is still hanging at the front of the room, and napkins congratulating Moira and Tom on reaching twenty-five years together are stacked on the table where the manager left us sitting.

"They're probably more worried about losing guests due to a break-in than us. I mean, I'm pretty sure they don't really give a shit about our safety," Heidi says once the manager leaves the room.

I roll my eyes. It's all I can do to stop myself from saying something that I'll later regret. For starters, Heidi's key card mysteriously went missing while she was out with Shiner Bock. Then, while we stood outside the door of our wrecked room, the person across the hall wandered out and drunkenly told us—through sloppy bites of loaded nachos that made my stomach turn—that the guy from last night had *just* left. It didn't take a detective to figure out that Heidi had been royally screwed over by Finn, the so-so one-night stand.

I hear footsteps coming in my direction, and I flick a wary gaze up from the blank police report to take in Officer Townsend, the police officer who answered the call. "Mrs. Martin—" he begins.

I cringe but quickly jump to correct him. "It's Kylie," I say, glancing up at him. Out of habit, I run my thumb over the last name tattooed around my ring finger. "Or Ms. Wolfe works, too. I never got around to changing my last name after my divorce." It was more than seven years ago, but I'm not about to tell him that.

A deep flush spreads around the crown of Officer Townsend's balding head. "I'm sorry about that, ma'am."

There's no need for him to apologize for calling me by my legal name, so I manage a ghost of a smile and shake my head.

When I drop my attention down to the sheet of paper sitting on the banquet table, Officer Townsend adds, "You'll want to call your credit card companies and let them know your cards have been stolen. You'll need to keep a copy of the report for your bank and a copy for your reference because it has your case number on it."

I slump in the folding metal chair. For a long time, I simply stare at the police report, letting the typed words blur together into a dizzying cluster of black and white. My brain is such a catastrophic mess from what happened in the laundry room with Wyatt to finding out my room was robbed that I didn't even think about taking precautions to make sure my bank account and my brother's business account won't be wiped out.

"Mrs. Ma—*Kylie*?" Officer Townsend takes the seat directly across from me, and I lift my face to his. "Do you need help filling out the report?" His heavy accent is gentle, but I shake my head.

"No, I'm fine, thank you." I pick up the pen to begin writing out my statement. It won't be much, considering I was bent over a running dryer with my jeans pulled around my knees while my room was being ransacked. As I scribble my signature and the date across the bottom of the page, I work my bottom lip between my teeth. "Can you show me what I'll need to do to follow-up on this?"

Officer Townsend spends the next few minutes showing me where my case number is located on the report and what phone number I'll need to call in order to check the status. When he's finished, he asks, "Will you be in the area for a while?"

I rake my hands through my blue-and-black hair, pulling it up into a stubby ponytail on top of my head before dropping the strands to fall around my face. "No, I'm heading back to Los Angeles in the morning."

The moment those words fall from my lips, I cringe, but Officer Townsend doesn't seem to notice. He's speaking to Heidi, explaining everything to her now.

Shiner Bock has my credit cards, which would be okay because I can get back home without my Visa or American Express. I've survived traveling without money before, and I can easily do so again. But when he cleaned out my room, he took everything in the nightstand drawer, including my ID.

I've had my entire makeup bag confiscated by TSA. There's no way in hell I'm getting through the gate tomorrow without my license.

Or renting a car.

Or boarding a Greyhound bus.

*Fuck.*

Clenching my teeth together, I amend my statement with Officer Townsend. "I *might* be going back to L.A., in the morning." My breath hitches, but I swallow down the anxiety, making myself continue. "My license is gone, so I don't think I have a way to get on my flight."

He gives me a sympathetic nod. "We're going to do everything we can to recover all your belongings, ma'am."

As Officer Townsend escorts us out of the banquet hall, so we can book a different room for the night, Heidi shoots me a pitiful look. "I'm so sorry, Ky," she whispers.

Since most of my initial irritation with her has evaporated, I lift the corner of my mouth and shrug. "Shit happens, babe. I'm just glad he wasn't dangerous."

My words must do her in because by the time we reach the entrance to the empty lobby, tears are streaming down her face, leaving dark eyeliner smudges that ruin the rest of her makeup. Miserably, I lower my brown eyes to the polished black floor just as I hear Wyatt call out to me from the concierge desk.

"Kylie?" The panic resonating in his deep voice causes my throat to swell. He reaches me in a few long sprints and yanks me to his muscular chest. Cupping the sides of my face between his large hands, he bends down, so our eyes are level. "What the fuck?"

I'm startled by how wild his blue eyes look, and I immediately blurt out, "I'm alright."

I dart my gaze to Officer Townsend and whisper a thank-you. He gives me a nod of his head before taking off to talk to the manager on duty. Heidi slinks off toward the front counter, looking behind her in my direction once before dropping her eyes to the floor.

Pushing my shoulders back, I turn my gaze to Wyatt, and he straightens, dropping his hands to my waist to encircle it. "I'm fine," I say once more.

He slightly loosens his hold on me, only moving his fingers to the small of my back. It's as if he's unable to let go, and I find it comforting. As he guides me toward the couches in the lounge area, I stay as close to him as our bodies will allow because, truthfully, I don't want him to let go of me either.

Not just yet.

"Don't put me through that shit again." His voice is hoarse. Before I'm able to respond, he continues, "I text you, on the right number this time, and I get nothing back. When I go to your room, a fucking cop is there, and still, nothing from you. And then these fuckers at concierge refuse to tell me what's going on."

"I was filling out a police report." We sit on the couch at the same time, and I accept his hand when he reaches for mine, linking our fingers. I tell him everything that's happened before and after we met up tonight, leaving out the part about the disastrous double date with Shiner Bock and James. "I honestly didn't even think to check my phone."

He brings our hands to his mouth, running his lips across the backs of my knuckles. My chest expands, my muscles relax, and I squeeze his fingers.

"Don't say sorry, Ky. Just don't fucking…scare me again."

*Wyatt McCrae. Scared.* Something about him admitting that to me tonight—on the night that we've agreed would be our last—sends multiple emotions pummeling through me, beating against my heart like a strong fist.

I pull out of his grip and scrub the heels of my palms over my eyes. "God, why do you have to say things like that *now*?" I drag my hands back, slicking tears through my hair as I push it away from my forehead.

A look of regret, which is quickly replaced by tenderness, flashes in his eyes. "Because it's true." He tugs me back to him, cursing. "And don't do *that*. I can take tears from anyone but you, Ky."

"I swear I'm fine." I feel a little ridiculous…okay, incredibly ridiculous. I've never actually cried in front of him because he's usually not around by the time the letdown kicks in and the waterworks begin. "I just need to go to bed."

I stand to go join Heidi at the front desk, but he closes his hand around mine. "You're not sleeping anywhere but with me tonight."

As much as I want that to happen, as much as I want him, I can't in good conscience leave my best friend alone. "I should stay with Heidi."

Wyatt's blue eyes scan the lobby until they zero in on Heidi. She's kicked off her stilettos and is leaning against the front desk with her eyebrows pulled together as she signs a receipt. She was lucky. When Finn ditched her in favor of raiding our room, she had her license and bank cards on her. Instead of going directly back to our room, she'd stopped for a pity party shot at the first bar she found. I hate to think of what would have happened if she came straight to The Veranda.

I hate to think of anyone hurting Heidi because she's right up there with my parents and Lucas and the band for me.

"I can't leave her alone, Wyatt," I say, my voice brimming with so much emotion that he draws his thick eyebrows together.

"I'm going to text Cal." He reaches into the pocket of his jeans for his phone.

I stop him, grabbing his hand, before he can send the other guitarist a message. "They hate each other."

The last thing I want is to hear Heidi and Cal bicker, and they've been doing it for years, ever since he hurt her feelings by turning her down after a show. A vicious migraine is starting to make my eyes burn, and I doubt listening to them angrily spit out douche bags, hoebots, and fucksticks every few minutes will make it feel any better.

"And?" Wyatt's smile is cocky and infuriatingly handsome. He shrugs out of my grip, his fingertips skimming mine in the process. He doesn't seem to care that I'm glaring flame-tipped darts into his forehead as he sends Cal a message. "At least she won't be alone."

"Your tenacity is unnerving."

"I want to do so many fucking things to you when you talk like that."

"Let me talk to her, okay?" Sighing, I start toward Heidi, turning around to glance back at him a couple times . His eyes follow me, doing a double take when they drag over my ass. He's probably just now realizing that I've not showered or changed since he left me, and knowing Wyatt, it's probably giving him more ideas. "You shouldn't look at me like that," I hiss over my shoulder.

"Why the hell not?" he drawls. Running the tip of his tongue over his bottom lip, he gives me a confident smirk. "Trust me, she'll say yes."

I turn to face Heidi, whispering under my breath, "We'll see."

But, in the end, Wyatt is right. Heidi feels like she's screwed up my night enough, so she doesn't want to ruin what I had planned. Without so much as an eye roll, she quickly agrees to sleep on the extra queen bed in Cal's room.

Wyatt and I go with her to grab her bags...well, bag because that's all that's left of her designer suitcases in our room. Most of my luggage is still there, and I pack my remaining belongings quickly. When Wyatt excuses himself to return to his suite, taking my stuff with him, I walk with Heidi to Cal's room on the sixth floor.

On the third knock, Cal flings open the door, wearing nothing but a towel. A toothbrush is in his mouth, and his black hair is clinging to his damp shoulders. Leaning against the door frame, he gives Heidi a head to toe once-over. While under his scrutiny, I feel her fidget beside me.

Through a mouthful of toothpaste, he says, "Your mascara looks like shit."

*And here we go.*

Heidi sneers. "I'm only staying with you because I love Kylie, limp dick." She shoves past him, snapping the towel away from his waist in the process.

I've been on the road with the guys so much that there's nothing I haven't seen, but I still cover my eyes, feeling heat creep up my neck.

He chokes on the toothpaste and garbles something.

I'm laughing as I back away from the door. After the night I've had, it feels good to laugh. "Good night, y'all."

Cal is still coughing when I begin to head down the hallway, but before I hear his door close, he says in a clear enough voice, "Bet you're not going to try your small-dick-phone-sex humiliation shit on me now."

\*\*\*

For the next forty-five minutes, I sit in the hotel's business center, canceling all my credit and debit cards. It's a pain in the ass because it's so late, but I finally get it done and order replacements to be delivered to my apartment in L.A.

By the time I'm ready to go upstairs to Wyatt's room, I'm so exhausted that I practically drag myself across the lobby, and I lean against the wall of the elevator as I ride up to the fifth floor.

The door to Wyatt's room is propped open with the hotel's binder that's filled with information about local restaurants and the cable channel lineup. I pick it up as I go inside, and then I lock the dead bolt and throw the binder on the chair by the door. I follow the hum of the pipes into the bathroom, walking into a haze of fog from the steam.

Wyatt pokes his head out from behind the shower curtain while he's scrubbing shampoo into his scalp. "You. Naked. In the shower. Now."

"You. Caveman. Go screw yourself." I shed my clothes anyway and kick them under the sink. I take his hand and carefully step into the shower. I recoil at how hot the water is, but he pulls me to him, shielding my body from the stream, as he adjusts the temperature.

"It took you fucking forever." He lathers soap over my breasts, testing the weight of each, as his thumbs trace around my nipples. His hands move to my belly button, and when he glides a soapy finger around it, I shiver. "Thought you forgot about me."

He's echoing my sentiments from earlier tonight, and I smile slightly. "No, that's impossible. I had to cancel my cards before someone steals all of Lucas's money, and he decides to strangle me."

"He's too busy with Red to notice anything, except for her pus—"

I flare my palms down his slick abs and his toned V to grab his cock. This must catch him off-guard because his lips part. "I don't want to hear things like that about my brother."

Wyatt laughs but then asks in a serious voice, "Did you get everything handled?"

"He stole my ID, too."

He bends his head, so he can run his tongue around my lips. "You know what has to happen, beautiful," he says. I start to move my fingers away from him, but he closes them back around his length. "You know that you're coming with me tomorrow, don't you?"

*Yes, I know.* I've known that's how things would go down the second Officer Townsend mentioned my credit cards, and I realized there was no way I could board my flight tomorrow. I study Wyatt's shit-eating grin. "You planned this, didn't you?"

"For some motherfucker to screw you over? No. But for you to come with me? Yes. That was my plan all along."

"And the fact that someone broke into my hotel room makes it easier for you."

He pins me against the shower wall, hitching my leg around his waist, and I let go of his erection, so I can grip his tattooed shoulders for support. Water is beating down on my face, but I don't blink as I wait for him to answer.

"Did you really think I'd give you up so easily, beautiful? Did you think I'd let you go without reminding you why you fucking fell in the first place?"

I swallow hard and nod.

Before he lowers his mouth to mine, he shakes his head in disappointment as he murmurs, "Then, you must not know a goddamn thing about me."

# CHAPTER SIX

Generally speaking, I hate the way the insides of rental cars smell. I don't know anyone who gets excited about the stale musk scent of dusty vacuum cleaner and Windex. But when I open the Suburban's passenger door early the next afternoon, I pause. And I inhale. This particular vehicle smells like Wyatt's cologne, Jean Paul Gaultier's Le Male. I bend and put my nose closer to the seat. This time, I breathe in the scent as deeply as my lungs will allow. He must have spritzed some all over the leather when he was loading our bags.

A shiver courses down my spine.

"Are you…" Heidi's voice coming up behind me startles me, and I jolt up to see her and Cal walking up to the Suburban together. As I shuffle away from the car, he gets inside, moving all the way to the back row, but Heidi doesn't budge. She raises her thinly arched eyebrows and slips her hands into the front pockets of her floral-print skinny jeans. "Holy shit, Kylie, you're sniffing the seat."

"No, I—"

But she pokes her head into the car and breathes in. "Ooh, that does smell good. Wonder what you're thinking about right now." She climbs into the Suburban through the back door and plops down in the middle seat, folding her skinny arms across her chest. Cal snorts from the row behind her, and even though her eyes narrow dangerously, she ignores him. "This will be fun," she says to me, a little too cheerfully.

Instead of holding back the nervous laugh building in my chest, I let it out as I slide my sunglasses over my face. There's nowhere near enough sunshine today to need the oversized aviators, but they'll help me sleep on the ride. At least, that's the plan.

"I sure as hell hope this'll be good," I say.

"There'll be music. What's not fun about music?" Heidi asks.

Cal says something to her from the backseat, and though I'm not a hundred percent positive, I'm pretty sure he said, "And the dicks attached to the guys who play it." Whatever it is was, it earns a hissed, "Fuck you," and the bird from Heidi.

Biting the inside of my cheek, I rub the back of my neck. I'm already dreading the fact that I'll be forced to listen to Heidi and Cal's back-and-forth until the end of the week, which is three days from now.

When I spoke to Heidi about my plans to travel along with Wyatt and Cal this morning, she promptly volunteered herself for the trip. I was quick to point out how unnecessary it is for her to spend her free time with me on the road, and of course, she was quick to argue, claiming that not tagging along isn't even an option.

*"You don't have to do that, babe. I don't have a choice, but you do," I tell her. "Catch your flight and get back to sexing up drunk guys."*

*She responds by ripping her itinerary into tiny pieces and dropping them into my hand. "You're stuck with me now."*

*"You do know that you can just print another one, right?"*

*Flipping her chestnut waves over her shoulder, she presses her lips together. "It's...what? Only four days, counting today? And it's not like the phones are going anywhere. It's my fault that you have to be with them, so I want to go."*

Though I should have, I didn't tell her the sad, twisted reality of it all.

A part of me is thrilled that I'm going along for the ride and ecstatic that I'll have these few extra days with Wyatt just so I can get everything off my chest. Even if he will be busy driving and performing the majority of that time, we'll have the opportunity that was taken away from us last night.

But then, a part of me aches inside because I know that prolonging my time with him will just slice open my heart a little more. He didn't tell me the exact plan for this trip until this morning, and when he did, I was speechless for a long time.

The first leg of our trip is the same route that we took eight years ago when I realized that I loved him. It's the same route where I went from the girl who coped with her insecurities by physically hurting herself to the woman who's spent the last several years carving deeper emotional wounds into her body.

Wyatt's breath on my neck separates me from my thoughts. I face him with a forced smile on my face.

"Ready?" he asks.

I tip my head back before I answer him, glaring up at the overcast sky through my sunglasses. "Yeah, I am." Taking a small step toward the car, I say, "But fair warning—if you end up asking me to chauffeur you around, I might break that pretty blue Kramer of yours over your head."

He inclines his head toward the back compartment of the SUV where his Kramer guitar is safely stored. "I'm not Lucas, beautiful." He grabs my waist firmly between his hands, and lifts me off the ground, placing me into the Suburban.

"I'm capable of lifting my leg high enough to use the step rail."

"Trust me, I know exactly how high those legs will go." Before he closes my door, he winks and says, "By the way, Ky, you couldn't hurt that pretty blue Kramer even if you tried."

Using the rearview mirror, I catch Cal and Heidi stifling laughter from their respective rows. "Stop encouraging his bull," I say a little too sharply. But at least they've found common ground. It just blows that it's in the form of the tension crackling between Wyatt and me.

Wyatt slams down into the driver's seat, pops open the biggest Monster Energy drink I've ever seen, and starts the ignition. He glances over at me, wearing a grin that's far too sexy. "Let's do this shit."

"Let's," I say sarcastically.

I'm silent as he pulls out of the hotel parking lot. Because he hates GPS, he has to turn around at a gas station a quarter of a mile up the road.

"Babe, you do know that Garmin isn't actually watching every move you make, don't you? It doesn't have a camera recording every messed-up thing you say. So, trust me, if you use the damn GPS, I swear everything will be alright."

He rubs his tongue up and down the labret in his lower lip as if deep in thought before gesturing to the folded piece of paper lodged into one of the cup holders. "If you insist, Ky."

My nose wrinkles up when he gives in so easily, but I say nothing as I unfold the paper, which turns out to be the location of the Houston hotel. I alternate between punching the address into the GPS and glancing at him. "Done."

"If a close-up of my dick ends up on YouTube, your ass is mine, Kylie."

"Didn't you already claim it as yours anyway?" I challenge in a voice quiet enough for only him to hear, and he nods slowly. "Ugh, just drive."

I sit back in my seat and press my forehead against the cold window, watching New Orleans fade away, as Wyatt speeds the Suburban onto I-10 toward Houston. I don't know if he planned the road trip like this on purpose, but if he wanted me to remember everything, he's succeeded.

Out of the corner of my eye, I glimpse at him. His blue eyes are glued on the road, and one of his hands is gripping the steering wheel so tight that I swear I'll hear the leather split apart at any moment. His expression is suddenly unreadable, and I wish like hell I knew why.

Silently, he reaches past the center console and creeps his hand across my lap, not stopping until his fingertips brush the inside of my left wrist. Gasping, I jerk away as if he's scorched my skin with fire. I close my eyes, and I can practically feel the way his hand closed around my wrist when we left New Orleans all those years ago. It was before Your Toxic Sequel— at the time, Falling Anarchy—made it big, and I was huddled up against him in the backseat of Sinjin's Ford Expedition. I can hear the words he whispered to me, just as clear and startling as ever.

*"Does Lucas know?"*

*"God, no."*

*He let go of my arm and moves his hand to my thigh, squeezing just a touch too hard. The pressure makes my heart race, but in a good way. This isn't the first time Wyatt McCrae has touched me, but I know from this moment on, I'll consider it the beginning. It's not an accidental brush or an awkward hug from my brother's best friend. This is something else entirely, and it's both confusing and intoxicating.*

*"So why the fuck do you do it?" he demands, catching me off guard.*

*I stare at him, open-mouthed, for what seems like an eternity. His midnight blue eyes study me with care, and he waits impatiently for me to give him a response. Sliding a strand of my hair behind my ear, I flick my gaze to the front of the vehicle, where my brother is deep in conversation with Sinjin. When I face Wyatt directly, I'm as honest as I can be.*

*"Because I'm not good enough. Because my parents have Lucas, and I can barely manage to—"*

*"You're everything. Don't believe for one second he's any better than you or that you don't deserve just as much love."*

*I start to speak, but he cuts me off. "Kylie, the cutting?" His voice is soft and dangerous, possessive and sexy, and I lean closer to him. "Don't ever fucking do it again."*

*I swallow hard. Fall hard. And I never look back.*

*"I promise I won't."*

I kept that promise, only wavering once since then.

Now, I open my eyes and make myself a new vow—to stay away from all these memories and make it back to L.A., without dredging up more of our history.

He rests his palm on my thigh, and I lower my brown eyes to it, relieved that I had the good sense to wear sunglasses. Dragging in a harsh breath of air, I cover his hand with mine.

\*\*\*

Heidi absolutely refuses to stay with Cal another night, and because I'm virtually broke and without an ID until I return to L.A., I agree to share a room with her when we reach the Onyx Hotel in Houston five hours later. With an atrium lobby and floor-to-ceiling windows, the place is far more luxurious than the hotel we stayed at in New Orleans. The Onyx also comes at an extravagant price, and Heidi has no problem letting us know during check-in.

"Could you have picked anything more expensive?" she asks Wyatt as she slides the front desk clerk her MasterCard. "I mean, I realize you make a gazillion dollars a year, and I think that's good for you and all, but some of us aren't famous."

Rolling his dark eyes, Cal grabs his bag and guitar from the floor. As he walks past us, he says in a voice loud enough for even the clerk to hear, "Guess you'll be pulling a double shift on the phone-fuck line, huh?"

Heidi takes her card from the clerk's outstretched hand, ignoring the look of mortification on the poor man's face, and she gives Cal a tight smile. "You've got my number, asshole. Just make sure there's enough money on your credit card."

"Please just bone it out of your system already," Wyatt growls under his breath, taking the words right out of my mouth. He works his way between them and grabs my bag and Heidi's. When none of us race to follow him, he glances back. "You coming?" His blue eyes linger on me for far too long when he says *coming*, and I don't miss the double entendre.

I linger behind to walk beside Heidi. "I'll pay you back when we get home, or I can get Lucas to Western Union you the money." *If I can even get in touch with him.*

My brother has been missing in action ever since Wyatt showed up in New Orleans, and I don't know if it's because he doesn't want to talk about Sin or if he's simply busy with Sienna. Sienna, on the other hand, has no problem answering my messages. She sent me multiple texts while we were on the way here.

Heidi waves her hand in the air, dismissing my offer to pay her for the hotel. "I can't take money from you."

"You *just* whined about the cost of the hotel."

"I whine about a lot of shit. It doesn't mean it actually bothers me."

I should have expected her to say this, but I still make a mental note to pay her back. I won't be able to sleep worth a damn at night, knowing I owe my closest friend.

Wyatt drops our bags in front of our door, which is thankfully on the first floor this time. He takes the key card from Heidi, pops open the door, and then scoots the luggage inside. Reaching out in her direction, he begins to place the card back into her hands, but then he pauses. He widens his stance and holds it over her head, earning a pissed-off glare from Heidi.

I cock an eyebrow and fall back onto the bed closest to the door. "She's on heels, McCrae, so please don't make her jump and break her neck."

While she's tapping her foot impatiently, he stares in my direction, drinking in the sight of me on the bed, as he tells her, "Please don't lose it this time."

Jerking the key out of his hand, she rolls her light blue eyes. "What time are you and Cal playing tonight?"

It's the first time I've heard her address Cal by his actual name.

Wyatt must also realize it because he grins. "I'll text Ky."

As soon as he leaves, she crawls onto my bed and collapses next to me. "You were so quiet the whole trip."

"You were asleep most of the time, and besides, I was tired."

I slept half the time on the way here, and the other half was spent texting back and forth with Sienna. She and Lucas are heading to my parents today as part of a documentary Lucas is taking part in, and she's worried my mom and dad won't like her. I told her the truth—if my parents accept and love Lucas and me with all our problems, then they'll love her, too. Of course, Sienna's messages also tell me that she and Lucas have obviously gone beyond the boundaries of professionalism.

"I'll be better after I get some sleep."

"But are you *okay*?" Heidi asks.

I *hate* the way she says *okay*.

My face is numb as I shake my head. "I'm a wishy-washy mess." I close my eyes and take a calming breath. When I glance at her again, Heidi's lips are curled down into a frown. She places her head on my shoulder, and we both stare up at the ceiling. "So, no, I guess I'm not okay."

"You will be."

I know that I will eventually, and it's for this reason that I bob my head slowly. "Thank you for coming with me." I smile tentatively. "Even if the reason for my vacation showed up, and things went to shit."

She grabs her chest theatrically and blinks back mock tears. "Thank you for still loving me after my douche bag one-night stand broke into our room and stole most of our crap."

My shoulders relax, and a couple seconds later, I'm laughing, and so is she.

"At least, I still have my iPod. I can play good music while I starve." As if on cue, my belly rolls. I skipped breakfast this morning, and I didn't pick up anything at the convenience stores along the way.

"And apparently you *are* starving." Heidi rolls onto her flat stomach and grabs a tall brochure off the nightstand. "Room service, it is." She knows me like the back of her hand because she orders me a cheesesteak and fries, my favorite. When she's done, she leaves my bed in favor of her own. As we wait for room service, she checks her voice mail to see if anyone from New Orleans has called about Shiner Bock.

They haven't, and after she hangs up I clear my throat, getting her attention. "Can I ask you a question?"

"You can ask me anything."

I bite my lip, hesitating, but when she nods her head to encourage me, I start, "You and Cal...have you ever—" My words are cut short when her face flushes bright red. My conflict with Wyatt is temporarily forgotten as I scramble into a sitting position. "You've got to be fucking kidding me!"

She lets her head loll off the bed. "Rock Fest, two years ago."

"And?"

"Your Toxic Sequel's show in Seattle last March."

"And last night?"

Snorting, she gives me a look. "Um, no. I was staying with him because the guy I slept with the night before broke into our room. Hooking up with Cal so soon after that would have been awkward not to mention an open invitation for all kinds of drama."

*Good point.* Still, with their outrageous bickering, I should have already known what was going on between them, and I mentally kick myself in the kneecap for failing to notice. "And you're just now telling me?"

She shrugs. "You never asked."

# CHAPTER SEVEN

It's eight thirty in the evening on the dot, and I'm dragging a striped, nautical print T-shirt over my head when my iPhone starts ringing from its spot on the dresser. "Shit," I snap as I shimmy the close-fitting top down my torso and over my belly button. Stepping over a small pile of Heidi's shoes, I snatch up the phone just before my ringtone, Chevelle's "I Get It," moves to my favorite part of the song, the line about living in an imaginary life.

I flip the phone right side up and mutter a soft curse when I see that it's my brother calling. After sliding my finger across the screen to accept the call, I tuck the phone between my ear and shoulder. "About damn time."

"I've been fucking busy, Ky. Sorry I haven't called you back." His voice is so strained that I immediately feel for him. "Besides, you said you wanted to be left alone while you were gone."

Before I left Nashville to go to New Orleans, I told him that I would quit if he so much as bothered me while I was away. I made a few more threats, but of course, he merely brushed them off.

"Since when do you give a crap whether or not I want to be left alone?"

"Since I decided I don't want to be bothered either."

*Well played, big brother.*

"Right…Sienna." I lean close to the mirror to determine if I want to spring for makeup tonight. One look at the dark smudges under my brown eyes is all the convincing I need. "How's that going?"

"She's good."

Leave it to Lucas to tiptoe around my question. He knows that I have a soft spot for her. There are few people I want to see at the receiving end of his bullshit, but Sienna's one of the people that I would actually step in front of to protect from my brother. I told Lucas as much when he first realized that he had a potential second chance with her.

"She's got everything taken care of here," he assures me.

*I bet she does.* "Don't fuck things up with her," I warn.

He sucks in a breath. "Jesus, Kylie, stop that shit."

I roll my eyes. "Yeah, I know. Stay out of your personal life. I get it."

When I hear a shuffling noise across the room, I look up to see Heidi in a giant robe, padding out of the bathroom. As she wraps a towel around her wet hair, her eyes find mine in the dresser mirror. She shifts one of her eyebrows curiously.

I turn my head around to face her. "It's my brother."

"Finally." She grabs her underwear and a bundle of clothes from her bed before returning to the restroom.

Focusing my attention back on Lucas, I ask, "How was the thing with Mom and Dad today?" While I wait for him to respond, I put my phone on speaker and leave it on the dresser, so I can finish getting ready. It's eight thirty-five now, and Wyatt and Cal's set with the band is supposed to start in twenty-five minutes. If I'm going to make it on time, I'll have to rush.

"It was alright, I guess. I mean, it's a fucking documentary about music. I don't really know *why* they wanted to talk to Mom and Dad, but I guess they were happy to see me."

Of course, our parents were happy to see him. Neither of us returns home to Atlanta enough, so my mother and father roll out the red carpet each time we decide to make an appearance. Compared to Wyatt, who rarely mentions his childhood or his parents, Lucas and I are fortunate. I didn't realize that for years because I had spent so long feeling like I was the kid my parents never wanted. I'd forced myself to believe that until I made myself physically sick.

But I'm lucky.

And I haven't smothered myself with that type of poison for a long time.

I clear my throat a few times, hoping it will relieve the tightness in the back of my mouth. "I'm so glad it went okay."

"Remind me why you wanted to let a film crew follow me around again," Lucas complains.

I can easily imagine the look on his face right now with his jaw clenched and lips pressed thin.

"Because it'll be good for your career." This isn't the first time I've told him that *Rock on the Road,* the documentary he's being featured in, would do nothing but help him, especially since Your Toxic Sequel is going on tour at the end of this coming summer.

"My career is fine."

I hear the squeak of his guitar followed by his sharp exhale. I tighten my grip on the pair of red skinny jeans that I plucked from my bag, bracing myself for whatever it is he's about to say.

"Mom wants to know what's going on with you."

"What? I'm fine." I sit on the edge of my bed and slide my pants up my legs. They're so tight that I have no other choice but to lie back to button them. "I'm really, really good in fact."

Lucas is always the first to pick up on my bullshit. It's an unnerving ability that he shares with Wyatt. They're both able to peel away my layers, go past the convincing smile, and figure me out. "What the fuck ever. She says you've been rescheduling trips back home since before Christmas."

Pushing myself up into a sitting position, I freeze, staring at the phone in horror at the thought of Lucas—who has a shitload of his own problems—and our mom having a lengthy conversation about me. "Did you tell her what I said? About coming to Atlanta for Easter?"

He snorts. "Yeah, I told them both."

"Well, then drop it. I keep my promises."

Maybe Lucas can hear the irritation in my voice, or he's just ready to get our conversation moving, so he can end the call. Either way, he changes the subject, transitioning easily to my vacation in New Orleans. "How was your flight back to L.A.?"

"God, do you check your text messages?" Doing a set of lunges toward my suitcase in hopes that my tight pants will loosen up, I say, "My flight was nonexistent." I bend over my bag and rummage around until I find my music note–print makeup case.

Lucas groans. "Don't make me play guessing games, Ky. What's going on?"

I toss the makeup onto the dresser and begin to pin my chin-length hair back from my face. "Some asshole robbed our room last night and stole my ID and credit cards."

"Fuck," he growls. Lucas surprises me then. Instead of immediately jumping down my throat and making sure that anything affiliated with him is safe, he goes into protective older brother mode. "You're not hurt, are you? He didn't touch you?"

My gaze lowers to the phone on the dresser, and I stare at it, rubbing my lips together. "If I didn't know any better, I'd say you're worried about me."

"Just answer the damn question."

"I'm fine. I was doing laundry when he broke in." *And banging your best friend in said laundry room.*

My brother releases a moan of relief. "So, what the fuck are you doing to get home? Do I need to send someone out there to get you? Do you need money to—"

"I'm fine." I'm grinning like an idiot as I dab concealer beneath my eyes. Lucas has his moments when I want to strangle him, but times like this remind me that he actually has a heart beneath his many layers of vice and all his growly impossible orders. "I've already scored a ride."

He doesn't respond, and there's nothing but silence between us. Since I hate silence and because I'm sure he's imagining me hitchhiking from New Orleans to L.A., with bearded men who call me Little Girl, I give in and tell him who I'm with. "Cal and Wyatt are bringing me home."

There's more quietness on Lucas's end because, apparently, his band mates are no better than random men.

"You called them to get you?"

"No," I say calmly. "They were already planning to drive from New Orleans to L.A."

"What the fuck for?"

My teeth sink into my bottom lip as my brow pulls together. *Lucas doesn't know about Wyatt's deal to perform with Cal's cousin.* Suddenly, this entire arrangement just screams shadiness. Even though I was not told by either Wyatt or Cal to keep my mouth shut about the shows, I skirt around the subject with my brother. "They're not entitled to a vacation?"

"To each his own." There's a sound on Lucas's end of the line, like he's rubbing his hand over his face. "One, I'm going to find that little shit who robbed you and break his fucking legs. And two, I'm going to call Wyatt."

I grip the handle of my mascara, and when I stare at my reflection in the dresser mirror, I realize that I'm holding it like a weapon. "I don't need you to baby me, Lucas. I can take care of myself."

"Oh, I know you can, but it still won't stop me from calling him," my brother says in a rough voice. I hear Sienna murmur something to him in the background, and he releases a low noise of frustration. "You be good, Ky. I'm going to get off here."

I try not to think about the multiple meanings behind those particular words. "Hey," I say quickly before he has a chance to hang up. Lucas pauses. "Sinjin? How's everything going with him?"

He's quiet for a long stretch, contemplating exactly what to say next. I drop the tube of mascara on top of my makeup bag. My hands are already shaky enough as it is. If my brother says something that'll piss me off, the last thing I want to do is poke myself in the eye.

"I think he's going to be alright this time."

"You said that the last time." And we argued about it that time. In fact, Lucas was so moody about me confronting him and acting like he didn't care enough that he handled all his business transactions himself for a week before finally caving and apologizing to me.

"Yeah, well, I think this is it. He scared himself."

Lucas leaves it at that, but I understand what he's saying.

Even before Wyatt confronted me about the cutting eight years ago, I was determined to stop. I was afraid of where my mission to cope with all my shortcomings—no, what I *felt* were my shortcomings—through little slices of pain would take me. I knew that I was messed up, and more than anything, I wanted to fix myself. But even determination has boundaries, and I'm still thankful that Wyatt McCrae caught me before I could break through those.

Heidi pokes her head out of the bathroom door. "Hey, ask him if he knows Sin's address." Once again, she disappears, and the soft roar of the hotel's blow dryer kicks in.

Lucas doesn't have the exact address, but he tells me the name of the rehab, which I jot down using a blue eyeliner pencil and the back of a pizza flyer. Then, he says he needs to go help Sienna arrange an appointment for tomorrow morning. Considering it's close to ten in Atlanta, it's, without a doubt, the lamest excuse I've ever heard.

"Have fun with that," I say dryly. I start to ask him how things are going with her just to see if he'll give me a straight answer this time, but then I decide against it. He's anxious to get back to her, and that tells me he's getting his way. I just pray he treats her right.

Lucas ends the call on a positive note. His "I love you" makes my head reel. I sink down on the edge of my bed, tapping my fingers together anxiously, until Heidi comes out of the bathroom and calls me out.

"Kylie?"

I lift my gaze to her. She's managed to coax her curly hair straight, and she's dressed simply, wearing dark jeans and a red silk bustier that my boobs could never pull off. She's also frowning at me.

"Why are you staring at a blank TV screen?"

"My brother just said he loves me."

She shrugs, undaunted. Heidi has four brothers, and *I love you* is a phrase that's common in her house. Don't get me wrong. My mom and dad are quick to tell me that. But Lucas? Not so much.

"That's a good thing, right?" she asks.

Pressing my palms into the mattress, I push myself to my feet and return to my makeup. "I think he's falling for Sienna."

Heidi slides into the chair on the far side of the dresser and begins rubbing Victoria's Secret lotion on her bare arms. "The chick filling in for you? He's known her for...what? Maybe a total of three weeks if you count whatever happened between them a few years ago?"

I brush bronzer across my cheeks and shake my head. "Doesn't matter. Lucas doesn't act like this. Ever." As I drag the hairpins out of my hair, I catch Heidi's face draw into a network of worried lines. I can only assume she's thinking about my brother's ex-wife, and I swallow hard. "Yeah, I'm hoping it works out, too."

"Sam's been quiet lately. Maybe she's gotten over him."

*Or Lucas is paying her off again.*

I force a smile as I turn to face Heidi and then twist around in a slow circle. She rakes her eyes over me before giving me a slow nod of approval.

"Ready?"

"We're late," she points out as we leave our room. After I slide into my jacket, she squeezes my shoulder reassuringly. "Hey, stop worrying about your brother. He's a big boy, so you don't have to play relationship police. Samantha's crazy ass has probably moved on, making some poor loser miserable."

For Sienna and my brother's sake, I hope Heidi is right.

\*\*\*

Since Wyatt and Cal are long gone, and at this point, probably playing the second or third song of their set, Heidi and I walk the four blocks from our downtown hotel to the bar, huddled up close to each other despite the muggy Houston night. I don't even think about my missing license until we're about to be carded at the entrance, but then a willowy blonde with giant green eyes, who reminds me of Taylor Momsen from The Pretty Reckless, sidles up to the door supervisor.

"It's alright. They're with the Toxic Sequel boys," she says in a husky voice. Raking her hand through her platinum hair, she winks a heavily lined eye at me. "Heidi and Kylie, right?" When I nod slowly, cocking one of my eyebrows, she shrugs. "You're the only chick with blue hair who's come in all night. I've been keeping an eye out for you for Wyatt and Cal."

Moving aside, the bouncer jerks his head back into the bar, and Heidi and I step inside. Because it's already steamy in here from the friction of so many scantily clad bodies, I shed my jacket and ball it up under my arm.

"Thanks," I tell the blonde.

Her lips curve into a little smile. "Don't mention it. Wyatt said you lost your ID, and I'm pretty close to the staff."

It's impossible for me not to notice the way her voice slides over his name. It's the same way mine does when my legs are wrapped around his shoulders while my nails are digging into his back. I swallow hard but blame my sudden discomfort on thirst and the guy who accidentally bumps into me. "Glad he's looking out for me."

She tilts her head to the side, sizing me up, before she motions for Heidi and me to follow her. As she leads us through the throng of drinkers, she peeks back over her shoulders. "I'm Terra, Hazard Anthem's manager."

I'm not terribly old myself—only twenty-five—but Terra hardly looks old enough to be in this damn bar, much less be the band's manager. I nod anyway as I step over a puddle of what I *hope* is booze on the floor. She stops to talk to some guy who stumbles all over her. When he grabs her ass, I can't help but be a little envious. I modify my initial assessment of Terra.

*She's Taylor Momsen with Kim Kardashian's ass.*

"I want a drink," Heidi says loud enough to be heard over the screech of the guitar and the lead singer, who is a screamer and a damn good one. "Want me to grab you something?"

"Corona?"

"You got it, babe. Get us a table?"

I slink away from Terra, who's still in deep conversation with the groper, and find a spot close enough to the stage to get a good view of the band but far enough away so I won't have groupies bumping into me every five seconds. When Wyatt's eyes meet mine, he grins and winks. He strokes the tip of his thumb over the neck of his Kramer in a slow, deliberate movement meant to make me think of his fingers between my legs.

He succeeds.

"So, you're Lucas-Fucking-Wolfe's baby sister?" Terra slips into the seat meant for Heidi.

I give her a polite smile. "Unfortunately."

"I met him once...in..." Terra darts her green eyes upward, trying to recall the exact location, and then she lowers her gaze, grinning. "2010."

"At your high school graduation party?" I mean to keep that to myself, but somehow, it slips out.

She's obviously not offended because she throws her head back and laughs.

"Rock Fest, but I'm pretty sure I'm older than Lucas and Wyatt."

She says Wyatt's name the same way she did at the door—with that desperate hush of admiration mixed with desire. I glide my tongue from side to side between my teeth. *Plenty of women are attracted to Wyatt McCrae.* There's no reason whatsoever for me to have a negative reaction to this particular one just because she can appreciate a sexy, talented man.

Heidi's hand reaches down over my shoulder, plunking a Corona with lime down in front of me. "Here you go, love." I glance back at her just in time to see her give Terra a long look that's one part curious and the other part aggressive. "Sorry, did you want me to grab you something, too?"

Sliding out of Heidi's chair, Terra shakes her head. Her mane of blonde hair flies around her face like a slow-motion shampoo commercial. "I've got..." She flicks her green eyes toward the stage. "Band stuff to do, but I'll catch up with you bitches later." She winks again.

Somehow, Heidi holds in her snort until she's out of earshot. "She's cute." She takes a swig of her banana bread–flavored beer. I'm a big fan of trying new flavors, but I can't help but wrinkle up my nose at the bottle. "Bet she gets them a bunch of gigs."

"Maybe." I focus my eyes back to the stage. The band has changed songs, and now, they're playing a metal version of Heart's "Crazy on You" that literally gives me chills. It's a feeling that very few bands have been able to bring out in me, and I've got a good feeling about Hazard Anthem's future. "They could probably be managed by a fucking ogre and still hit it big."

As my gaze skims back over Wyatt, I bite the inside of my lip. He's sweaty from the heat and exertion. When he's in his element like this, playing incredible music, it takes my breath away.

With a thoughtful look on her face, Heidi runs her finger in a circle around the neck of her beer bottle. "You think that's why Cal and Wyatt are helping them out? I mean, you don't think they're thinking about leaving Your Toxic Sequel, do you?"

Wyatt told me before that he has no plans to leave the band, so I decide to take him for his word. "I think YTS will be alright."

She breathes a relieved sigh before twisting around in her seat to watch the band perform. She taps her fingers on the table, singing along with the lyrics but getting seventy-five percent of them wrong. "You're right. They are kick-ass," she says once the song ends.

My sight is still connected with Wyatt's midnight blue eyes as I murmur, "Absolutely amazing."

# CHAPTER EIGHT

My appreciation for Hazard Anthem's music only grows over the next hour during the band's seven-song set. The lead singer has a range that reminds me of M. Shadows, and I find myself developing a bit of a voice crush on him. The band performs a little of everything from the angst-filled and powerful to a couple more covers to even the upbeat innuendo-laced music that put Your Toxic Sequel on the map.

The moment their set is finished and they've torn down their equipment for the next band, the lead singer maneuvers through the crowd in our direction, seemingly oblivious to the female hands grasping at various parts of his body. Before I can say a word, he jerks me into a hug.

When I go entirely still, he pulls back a little, narrowing his dark eyes. "Ah shit, please tell me you're Kylie."

"Yeah, I am."

He wraps his arms around me again, and Heidi makes a face at his back. "I've been wanting to meet the infamous Kylie Wolfe since Cal started playing with YTS."

"You're his cousin?" It's a stupid question. They look similar, except this guy is built and has short, spiky black hair as opposed to Cal's lanky stature and shoulder-length locks.

"Nate Romero," he says. When his dark eyes brush over Heidi, he grins. "You must be—"

Since none of us know exactly what Cal has told his cousin about Heidi, she clears her throat. "Heidi Wright. Nice to meet you." She lifts her chin slightly to take in Cal, who's walking toward us and clutching two bottles of some specialty beer.

"What?" Heidi's voice has dropped to the low, seductive purr she no doubt uses on her customers. "No PBR tonight?"

Cal's lips jerk into a grin. "Fuck you, Heidi."

"You were right." When Nate glances back at his cousin, I swear Cal's olive complexion goes scarlet. "She *is* fucking hot." He dips his attention back down to me. "I'd tell you the same, but McCrae would fuck me up in the parking lot."

*Wyatt has mentioned me.* In a way, it makes Nate assume that we're a couple.

*Good God, what has been said about me?*

I pull at the neck of my T-shirt, stretching out the tip of the sequin anchor on the nautical print. "Where's your drummer?" I peek around the crowd in search of the bald man who was on stage up until a few minutes ago. As much as I hate to admit it, his skill is almost as mind-blowingly good as Sinjin's.

Nate turns and scans the area before he finally points to the far corner of the bar. "Ben's over there with Terra and Wyatt," he says. Of course, hearing that Terra's with Wyatt makes my stomach clench. Looking back at me, Nate mistakes my abrupt smile for something else—anticipation. "You wanna go over?"

I consider this for a moment, but then decide against it. There's a nearly full bottle of Corona on my table—my fourth drink in the last hour—and I've gotten to the point where I've started to want to hug the bottles. "Maybe in a few." I jab my index finger toward the small group of women who've edged their way up to Cal. One is glancing in Nate's direction, tapping the cap end of a permanent marker against her hip. "I think you're being summoned."

I want to advise him that he's going to need more security soon, that there should already be more security since my guys are playing, but I stop before I say anything. I remind myself that I'm here as a music lover and not my brother's assistant.

Nate flushes, racking up a few more good points with me because he obviously hasn't let this world go to his head yet. "Looks like I am. See you in a little."

When I shimmy back onto my seat, Heidi casts a sharp look in my direction.

"What?" I ask.

She runs her thumb around the neck of the bottle she's been nursing for twenty minutes. "We're going over there."

I put my Corona to my lips and tip it back, drinking it entirely too fast. My nose is burning when I slap the empty bottle onto the wooden table. "If you feed me that bullshit about claiming Wyatt, I'm probably going to—"

She cuts me off. "Hey, Kylie." I press my lips together, waiting for her to continue. "You need to get your tipsy ass over there and claim Prince Albert."

"He got rid of that," I say through clenched teeth.

"Whatever. Point is, you've said it yourself, that this is it for you guys, that you're done with the games once we go home. So, why the fuck are you just sitting around and wasting the time you have left?"

This is another reason why Heidi and I get along. I'm not close to many women because I've felt the bitter sting of disloyalty, and it's left a foul taste in my mouth, but Heidi tells me like it is. She doesn't hold anything back even when her thoughts are all over the place.

"I'm not tipsy," I tell her.

She stands and adjusts her tight jeans. "And I'm not sober, Ky." She grabs my hand, hauling me off in Wyatt's general direction. As she passes Nate, Cal, and the women they're mingling with, she skims her hand across the crotch of Cal's jeans.

He stiffens and screws up signing the R at the beginning of his last name on the breasts in front of his face.

Wyatt's eyes drink me in long before I step into his bubble. "Bluebird." His hands touch the first thing he can grab, my forearm, and he brings me to his side. This is such an intimate gesture that my lips part slightly. Completely hypersensitive to my every move, his head bends a little. "You're fucking me up again," he says so softly that only I can hear him.

*Right. And he's not doing the same thing to me?* As his delicious scent of cologne mixed with sweat teases my nose, I dart my tongue across my lips. Before I can make a fool of myself, I glance away from him to Hazard Anthem's drummer. "Your sound is incredible."

Wyatt's mouth moves against my ear, and I can feel his labret slide up against one of my earrings as he opens his mouth to say something. I go perfectly still because I know he's about to say something that will result in him owning my panties by the end of the night.

Then, he pulls away, grinning suggestively. As he introduces me to the drummer, I realize he's thinking of a hundred creative ways to fuck me in this bar, and it sends a thrill of pleasure through me.

"You've already met Terra, but this motherfucker is Ben Dillinger. Ben, this is Kylie and Heidi." Wyatt jerks his head from me to my best friend, who's standing a couple feet away, typing something into her phone.

Ben, who's short and muscular with a shaved head, lifts his chin a little, acknowledging us. "Good to meet you," he says to Heidi as she slides her phone into her bag.

She takes his outstretched hand and gushes over how much she loved the set. Then, she excuses herself and struts away, her mission to find Cal obvious.

Ben turns to me. "Been wanting to meet you since this shithead joined up with us in Albuquerque last year."

This catches me off-guard, and I'm unable to keep a frown from making a momentary appearance across my face. *When did Wyatt go to Albuquerque? For that matter,* why *did Wyatt go to Albuquerque?* I dart my eyes up to him quickly, but he's focused on something else. *Typical dick move, Wyatt.*

Because I can feel Terra's enormous green eyes burning into me, I steer the subject in a slightly different direction. "You're playing there in two nights, right?"

As Ben bobs his head, a tiny pierced woman with a shock of platinum and jet-black hair slips between us. She murmurs, "Excuse me," and then slides a shot glass into Ben's hand. After he downs the amber-colored liquid, he gives her one of those looks that makes me melt. It's the look that's not only full of desire but also that chaos-free kind of love that I crave.

"Thanks, babe," he says.

She grins and wipes her fingers down the front of her ripped jeans before holding out a hand to me. "I'm Ivy, Ben's girl."

I grasp her hand, surprised at how firm her grip is. "Kylie Wolfe. Good to meet you."

I can't help but like Ivy because instead of mentioning my connection with Lucas, she immediately replies, "You play pool?"

"I've played." And I have, just not well.

She inclines her blonde-and-black head to the opposite corner of the bar where a tall woman dragging on a cigarette ducks into a dimly lit room. "Play with me?" She jerks her thumb from Ben to Wyatt. "You and me against them."

"Ky always loses," Wyatt tells her. He bites the corner of his lip when I glare up at him. "But fuck yeah, you're on. You in, Bluebird?"

I glance around the bar in search of my best friend, but she's nowhere to be found, and neither is Cal. I lift my shoulders. "Guess I am."

I quickly learn that Ivy's a bit of a pool shark and a whole lot competitive. She easily makes up for everything that I lack in the game, which is a lot unfortunately. She sinks billiard ball after ball into the table pockets. Each time, she rubs our winning streak in Wyatt and Ben's faces while pumping her fist to the raunchy anthem about getting drunk and waking up naked that's blasting from outside the poolroom. I'm ecstatic when I manage to knock one, the red 3, into the hole.

Between games, Wyatt has disappeared to get himself a drink, and Ben is talking to some of the band's fans, the three women who stalked Cal and his cousin for signatures a little earlier.

"You going to Albuquerque with them?" I ask her.

Ivy downs her Jagerbomb and shudders from the aftereffect. She rubs her hand back and forth over her mouth, bothering the hoop at the end of her nose, before she shakes her head. "No, I live in Katy, half an hour from here, so I can't go." She stares longingly at the empty shot glass and sighs. "Plus, I've got work in the morning. Guess I should've thought about work before I dived into the Red Bull, huh?"

"Nah. I mean, just drink a few more, and you should be good." I lean against the pool table, sliding my bottom up to the edge. Cocking my head to the side, I take in the women crowding around her boyfriend. "How long have y'all been together?"

"Four long-ass years." She glances over at Ben, who's signing right above one of the girl's lower back tattoos. "Wonder if she realizes how long it takes to get Sharpie off."

If watching other women fawn all over Ben fazes Ivy, she doesn't show it. She seems entirely at ease with the multiple sets of breasts being shoved in his face, and I find myself studying the obvious trust she has for him, asking myself how the hell she does it.

Even though Wyatt and I have promised not to lie to each other—and there have been those times when he's been so brutally honest that my chest aches for days—I've always hated the doubt that comes along with what he does for a living.

My thoughts are still conflicted when Ben and Ivy drop out of the next game, and Terra and Nate take their place.

"Wyatt says you sing," Nate says shortly after the new game begins. "Here, like this." He comes around the pool table and leans over me to reposition my grip on the pool stick. He's careful not to touch the intimate parts of my body, keeping his crotch several inches from my ass, as he guides my arm forward. "You wanna get up there with us during the next show?"

"Yeah, I sing…in the shower." I glance back into his teasing wide-set eyes. "And I'd ruin your show, babe."

"Bullshit," Wyatt says from across the table. When I lift my head, I flinch at how hard his eyes are despite the laughter in his deep voice. "She's goddamn amazing—everything about her is—but she's even better on the guitar."

"You play?" Nate asks, standing upright.

During the tour that changed everything for us eight years ago, Wyatt showed me how to play on Lucas's old Gibson. I've always been a quick study, so I picked it up easily. I'm not horrible, but I don't think I'm *goddamn amazing* either. Besides, I haven't played in well over a year.

"She's better than Lucas's ass," Wyatt answers for me, his tone a little mocking.

Jamming the bottom of my cue stick to the floor, I straighten my back and narrow my eyes at him. Other than with my ex-husband, this is the first time in years when Wyatt's played the jealous card around me. Because his intentions are obviously not to get me into his bed, Nate doesn't notice Wyatt's sudden mood change, but Terra does. She's standing on the far left corner of the table, taking in the exchange, as she slides the tip of her tongue back and forth between her lips.

"Actually, I haven't played in so long that I think I've forgotten how," I say.

Wyatt glides his pool stick forward, managing to knock the cue ball into a red stripe ball. It stops a mere few inches from the pocket. He straightens and glowers across the table at me. "You forgot?"

My shirt has crept up on my waist, so I pull it back down before I focus my gaze on Wyatt. I nod slowly and deliberately. "Yeah, I did."

Our eyes never waver away from each other even as Nate and then Terra take their respective shots. By the time it's his turn again, Wyatt slams his cue stick into the rack by the wall, and then he turns to me and jerks his head toward the door leading to the bar.

"Be right back," I tell Nate.

Terra answers quickly, beaming at both Wyatt and me with her megawatt smile, "We'll be here."

Wyatt's fingers close around my wrist, and as soon as we're out of earshot, he mutters, "There's no way in hell you're going anywhere tonight other than my bed, Kylie."

*Yeah, we'll see about that.*

Ivy stops me halfway across the bar. She's already wearing a jacket, and she yawns as she wraps a fringed scarf around her delicate neck. "I've got to go, but friend me, okay?"

After I get her last name and tell her that I will, I follow Wyatt into a quiet nook located in the other corner of the bar. It looks like it used to be a spot for pay phones, but now, there's only a dirty ashtray and a crumpled Winston Lights package.

"You trying to drive me crazy?" Wyatt bends his head, leaning in close to me, with his nostrils flared. When his short wheat-blond hair brushes the top of my forehead, I automatically reach up to touch it. "You trying to see what kind of rise you can get out of me?"

I jerk my hand away from his hair. "By what? Playing a game of pool? Abso-fucking-lutely not."

He stares at me for a long time before shaking his head. "I'm taking you back to my room, and then I'm fucking you until the only thing you can think about is me."

It's not necessarily his jealousy that makes me want to strangle him. It's the fact that he's already the only thing I think about, and he doesn't realize it. "I'm going to find Heidi." I start to walk around him, but he swings me back around.

"Heidi and Cal are long gone. It's just me and you, just like it's always been. Why the fuck don't you get that, beautiful?"

His words snip a nerve—and believe me, it's sharp and just a little excruciating—but I grab his forearm and stand my ground. "If you don't let go of me, I will headbutt you in your perfect teeth, McCrae."

He doesn't seem to care because his lips come down hard on mine, and his tongue is just as rough. Almost effortlessly, he shrugs out of my grip, and his hands travel to the sides of my back and slide into my jeans, pushing down my flimsy panties, so his skin is against my skin. "I hate this."

"Touching me?" I demand breathlessly. "Because, trust me, you don't have to."

"No, wanting to fuck-up every man who touches you. It's—
"

"I don't know whether to be flattered or freaked out that you're so jealous," I say.

He releases a sound and rests his chin on top of my head, but I'm so heated that I can't bring myself to return his embrace.

"Come back to the hotel with me."

"Why? So, you can beat up the front desk clerk when he looks at me for longer than ten seconds?" I start to ask him if he's planning to challenge my gynecologist to a parking lot duel, but I stop as his hands travel from their spot on my ass to the inside of the front of my red jeans. Despite how tight my pants are, he manages to maneuver his fingers between my legs. I gasp, tightening my thighs, but it's no use.

He's already found what he needs in the form of my damp panties. A self-assured smile builds on his face. "Because of that. Because no matter how pissed you are right now, your pussy still wants me."

I grip his wrist and tear his hand out of my jeans, trembling when his fingertips drag over my clit in the process. Wyatt thinks he has me figured out. He thinks that just because my body responds to him, I'll fall into his bed tonight, and I'll get over him being a dick.

This time, when I step around him, he doesn't stop me because he's certain I'm ready to go back to his hotel room. He's certain we'll end the night with angry sex and start the morning with it, too.

So, it must be a shock to his system when I say, "Have a wonderful night, McCrae. Let's try this again in the morning when you're not planning on taking your frustrations out on my girlie bits."

***

When I let myself into my empty hotel room half an hour later, I tumble into bed, and it's a shame that my thoughts are still focused on the way his hands felt.

# CHAPTER NINE

Shortly after four thirty the next morning, I hear a key card slide into the lock to my room. I'm still so wired from the night before that I've yet to fall asleep. The slight clicking noise on the other side of the door makes the hairs on the back of my neck stand on end. Fully alert, I slide myself into a sitting position and grab the first weapon I can find—my boot. After what happened back at the hotel in New Orleans, no one can blame me for being on edge.

My fear quickly dissipates when Heidi creeps into the room, holding her pumps to her chest with one arm, as she eases the door gently shut behind her with the other. She turns around and starts tiptoeing across the floor, but then she freezes as I flick on the lamp between our beds.

"Well, hell, I thought you'd be tied to McCrae's bed or something right about now."

I toss the clunky shoe down on the floor. "Surprise, babe."

She drops her shoes and kicks them, one by one, beneath the desk. "So, why *aren't* you in McCrae's bed?" She wrinkles her nose. "Is everything alright?"

Bringing my knees up to my chest, I circle my arms around my shins. I've spent the last several hours lying in the dark, my brain pinging between needing Wyatt and wondering whether or not everything will be fine with him until we return to L.A. I've yet to come up with a solution to either.

But to Heidi, I tip my head. "We're good. We have to leave so early that we decided to call it a night."

She pauses for a few seconds, like she's about to say something earth-shattering, but then she unzips her strapless top and pulls it off. Rolling my eyes, I glance away from the pierced boobage on display until she clears her throat. When I turn my head back to her, the red silk bustier is draped over the back of the chair, and she's stretching a tank top down her waist.

"You don't think I'm stupid enough to believe that, right?" She loops a ponytail holder through her dark hair, which has started to frizz.

I rub my hands up and down my legs. "Not at all, but I think you're smart enough not to make a big deal out of it."

"Oh, I am." She pulls off her jeans and tosses them on top of the red top before she climbs into bed. Adjusting her pillows, she looks up at me from beneath her long lashes. "And before you start making a big deal, no, Cal and I did not sleep together."

Stretching my legs back down the sheets, I flex my feet and hold up my hands defensively. "I wasn't even going to bring it up."

"You were thinking it. We just went to a few more bars." She grabs the remote from the nightstand, but before she switches on the flat screen TV, she cocks her eyebrow. "You tired?"

*With thoughts of Wyatt still strumming their way through my brain? Hardly.*

For an hour, Heidi and I sit in complete silence, which is a feat for us, considering we both loathe quiet situations. The only thing she finds worth watching is a rerun of *Game of Thrones* that she's probably seen no less than ten times. Midway through the episode, she crawls to the bottom of her bed, lies on her stomach, and refuses to look away from the TV, acting as if she hasn't already witnessed her favorite character's death.

"I hate this scene," she whispers. "I'll never watch this show again. *Never*. It rips out my fucking heart."

"You said that last year."

After the end credits play, she turns off the TV and blinks, her head lolling forward a bit. She's seconds away from passing out. Then, I'll be up alone, thinking about shit that I shouldn't, like thoughts that I would have been over by now if I didn't accept Wyatt's deal back in New Orleans.

Heidi returns to the top of her bed and stretches out on the pillows. Though her eyes are closed, she turns her head in my direction. "Do you think this is actually it for you and McCrae?"

"Yes," I say too quickly. The muscles in my face stiffen, but I continue. "Maybe. At some point, we have to stop trying if it's not going anywhere." Wyatt and I had reached that point a long time ago, but I didn't realize it until last year, a couple of weeks after our Thanksgiving Day hookup.

"You said that last year," Heidi says sleepily, repeating my earlier statement.

*Yes, but this year is different.*

Although Heidi is probably planning on having a ten-hour sleep marathon, her chances of accomplishing that are cut short when Wyatt shows up to our room a little after nine. He leans against the door frame, his body relaxed, as if we didn't argue last night.

I match his nonchalance and give him an easy smile that's the complete opposite of how I'm feeling. "Morning," I say.

He glimpses over my head and snorts when he eyes Heidi passed out on her bed, curled into a fetal position and breathing heavily. "Did you get my text?"

"Turned off my phone."

"Avoiding me?"

I lick the corner of my lips. "Dodging drama."

He curls his hand into the hem of my shirt and inches into the room, closing the space between us in a series of deliberate short steps. The sound of his boots dragging across the carpet is loud enough to mask the deep breaths I'm taking.

"Drama's not all bad, beautiful."

Shaking my head, I stare him down. "It is when I end my night wanting to murder you."

Wyatt's gaze lowers. His eyes are intense, unblinking, and the apology that I want from him is there, clearly visible behind the turbulent blue depths. I'm just not sure if it's enough.

"We're leaving in an hour." His fingers creep beneath my tee, splaying out on the smooth skin just below my belly button.

I mirror his movements, pressing my palms on the sides of his abs. "I'll wake Heidi up."

As he drops his mouth a little closer to mine, his warm breath fans across my face, and I tilt up my chin. "Not yet." His fingers trace the length of my torso, all the way up to the sensitive spot beneath my breasts, and then they move back down, cupping the wide curves of my hips. "You're still angry."

*Why does he have to make everything so difficult? Why does he have to tear me down at every turn just to make me want him at the next?* "Of course I am," I hiss, suddenly out of breath. "You acted like a jealous idiot."

The muscles in his neck tighten. "And you haven't?"

I lower my chin, scowling up at him from beneath my lashes, which are still coated in the mascara I used last night. "I've never insulted anyone speaking to you in a bar, not even when it was anything *but* innocent."

He mutters a curse, and just when I expect him to get the verbal apology out of the way so we can be on our way, he surprises me. He picks me up, and he literally hauls me over his shoulder.

"Put me down," I warn.

Ignoring me, he moves out of the doorway and uses the toe of his boot to close the door quietly.

"Wyatt, so help me—"

"You'll what, beautiful? Hit me? Scream?" His pierced lips drag up into a wicked grin. "You know I love it when you do both."

Because I don't want to give Heidi the shittiest wake-up call ever, I don't scream at him. Instead, I rake my sorry excuse for fingernails up his back through his soft black T-shirt. When he chuckles, I can feel it vibrate through my body. "You think that'll stop me from talking to you?"

*No, because he's probably getting a boner from it.*

He doesn't let go of me until we're behind the bathroom door, and even then, he sits me on the beige granite countertop, locking my legs between his. I hit him in the chest, hard, but he doesn't budge.

"You're letting it all out now, aren't you, babe? First, jealousy, and now this?" I demand. "You must truly want me to experience everything you've got to offer before we go back to L.A."

Wyatt's hand inches up my back, finally tangling into the tousled hair on the nape of my neck. "I was out of line last night." When he tilts my head back a little, giving my hair a tug, a shot of pleasure pours through me, and I make a soft sound. He must take it for a sound of disgust because he drags his other hand through his hair. "I fucking overreacted, Ky. I've never done that."

"No," I say, squeezing my eyes shut. "You haven't."

"It's getting closer—us getting back to L.A. And this is the first time I've ever believed you when you said you're through."

I panic because I don't want to hear him talk about the end. I feel like a strong hand is clenching my heart, stopping it from beating just right. I smooth my hand up his chest to the hollow of his tattooed throat.

"Don't do that," I whisper. He starts to say something else, but I move my other hand into his jeans and wrap it around his cock.

It's a coward move, but I never said I was opposed to taking the easy way out sometimes. "Don't," I say once more, gripping him firmly.

I feel him go hard slowly beneath my touch. He slumps forward, placing his palm flat on the bathroom mirror behind me. "You're killing me."

Acknowledging what he's just said with a stiff nod, I stroke my hand up and down his length, pressing my thumb to the top of his shaft.

"Open your legs," he breathes into my ear.

My chest is rising and falling heavily, and I want him—*oh god, I want him*—but I press my lips together. "No."

"I need to touch your pus—"

I slide my fingers from his neck to his lips. "No."

His long legs go weak, and I use this opportunity to loosen their grip on my legs. I place my feet on each side of him, nudging his jeans and boxers down his hips. When I pull him closer to me by enclosing his body with my legs, he sucks in a harsh breath.

"Fuck." His fingertips find their way back to my hair. "Your nipples are hard, and I know you're wet. Lie all you want, Ky, but I can see that shit in your eyes. You can't tell me you don't want me to touch you."

I curl my other hand around his length, and the fact that all my fingers are on his cock, stroking and squeezing, causes him to tremble.

"No, I can't tell you that because I *am* wet. I do want you to touch me," I say breathlessly. He groans, his lip piercing teasing my ear. "But now's not the time."

He leans back, the smile on his face a mixture of pleasure and pain, as he shakes his head. "Of course it is, beautiful. It's always the time."

But he respects my wishes. He doesn't try to touch me as I guide him to an orgasm. He buries his mouth against my neck, releasing a low animalistic sound on my skin. As he starts to untangle his fingers from my hair, he backs away, but I jerk him toward me, skimming my hands over his muscular shoulders.

"Kiss me."

His tongue parts mine, thrusting into my mouth, punishing me for not allowing him to touch me. He sucks on my bottom lip and then my tongue, but it doesn't bother me. In fact, it's addictive. When he draws back, I'm slow to open my eyes.

He's grinning, but the look in his eyes drops a brick into my stomach. It's the look of bitter defeat. "We've made a mess," he says.

I don't fail to catch the double meaning. "Yeah," I say softly, "we have."

# CHAPTER TEN

After Wyatt leaves my room, I decide to wait to try and wake Heidi, so I take a long shower that would deplete all the hot water back in my L.A., apartment. By the time I'm done, I've managed to calm my nerves, the trembling in my legs have stopped, and I'm articulate enough to understand. I can look my best friend in the eye without raising her suspicions about what Wyatt and I did a mere fifteen feet away from her while she was sleeping.

I spend a solid ten minutes trying to coax her out of bed, and Heidi doesn't take the disturbance well. Eventually, I look up a Lady Gaga song on my phone.

Fifteen seconds into "LoveGame," Heidi jolts up with bloodshot eyes and her hair flying everywhere. "That's so fucked-up, Ky."

"We're leaving."

She fumbles under her pillow for her phone. As soon as she checks the time, her expression goes blank. "You're kidding."

"You can sleep on the way there," I promise. "Trust me, you'll be fine."

But a few minutes later, while she's packing her belongings, she's still irritable and drowsy. "This is bullshit." She grabs her outfit from last night from the back of the chair and tosses it onto the heap of clothing in her suitcase. "They're not playing in New Mexico until when? Tomorrow night?"

I roll a pair of my jeans into a compact bundle and slide them neatly into my bag. "Albuquerque is nearly a thousand miles away from here, babe. With traffic and stops, it's an easy fourteen hours." Thinking of it in hours suddenly makes my ass sore, and I grimace.

"I should probably call my parents and let them know we'll be in Phoenix on Saturday morning, huh?"

She straddles her bag between her slim long legs, squeezes it tightly together, and tugs at the zipper. If my phone wasn't on the other side of the room, sitting on top of the mini-fridge, I would record this.

Finally, the zipper gives, and Heidi stumbles back, glaring at it. "I hate packing."

"What you just did was disturbing on so many levels." I rise from my spot on the floor and check my appearance one final time in the mirror. The effect that Wyatt has on me is obvious, at least in my opinion, as I study my reflection. I'm able to look past the circles beneath my almond-shaped brown eyes to see how my cheeks are flushed and how my lips seem fuller from kissing him earlier. My hand shakes a little as I trace the outline of my mouth.

Heidi clears her throat. "And you call me disturbing." I see her reflection in the mirror as her head cocks to one side. She shuffles closer to me, stopping just a few feet away from the dresser. "So, about visiting my parents—yay or nay?"

Because she's studying me so carefully, I respond quickly. "You should probably go see them." I twist away from the mirror, facing her directly. "They'd be pissed if you came to town and didn't at least meet them for dinner."

"Probably," she agrees, making me wonder why she asked me in the first place. "I haven't been home since Christmas."

"Then, you should definitely go."

Of course, advising Heidi that she needs to visit her parents once we reach Phoenix for the last show makes me feel like shit.

Over the past two months, my mom's been good enough not to put pressure on me about coming to Atlanta, but sooner or later, her patience will wear out.

"I'm probably going to go home next month. To Atlanta," I say.

Heidi nods her head, a smile of approval flitting across her glossy lips. "Good. I would invite myself, but you're probably afraid I'll meet some loser who'll steal your parents' car or something."

Rolling my eyes, I shove myself away from the dresser and bend down to zip my luggage. It closes on the first try without taking as much effort as it did her. "Stop giving yourself such a hard time." I sling the heavy bag over my shoulder, and I start coughing when it knocks the wind out of me.

Heidi's already waiting at the door, and once I catch my breath, I join her.

"You look thrilled," she says in a dry voice.

"Is it wrong that I don't want to do this today? You'd think I've never had to sit my ass on a tour bus for days at a time," I mutter.

"See, told you it was too damn early for this." She twists around to give me a sympathetic look, curling her bottom lip. "I'm going to sound like a complete tool, but it's not too much longer until we're home."

I'm right on her heels as she leaves our room, but I take one final peek inside before I let the door close behind us. I've left too many personal belongings in hotels across the country not to be cautious.

"And once we're back, I get to do this all over again, except I'll be taking orders from Lucas." My voice is sarcastically chipper.

Heidi stops in the middle of the hallway, earning a frustrated glare from the housekeeper who's trying to maneuver an oversized cart stacked high with cleaning supplies and toilet paper. I grab my friend's bony elbow and guide her out of the way.

As soon as we get to the staircase that leads down to the parking garage, she confronts me. "You're not fed up with your job, are you?"

I jog down the steps, taking them two at a time, so I'm out of breath by the time I reach the bottom. "I love my job."

Still, for the first time since I started avoiding Wyatt near the end of last year, I'm wondering how working for Lucas is going to affect me once I'm back in L.A. *Isn't the proximity and common ground the precise reasons why I let Wyatt back into my life time and time again?* Even if I can go through with cutting him out this time, every moment we're together, even the toxic ones, I know I'll doubt myself.

When I open the door to the parking garage, Heidi stops me, flattening her hand against the metal, as she slams it shut. "Ugh, the look on your face right now." She shakes her head, pressing her lips together, as if what she's looking at is the most pitiful thing she's ever seen.

Maybe, just maybe, it is.

"Heidi," I warn. "I'm not doing this with you today."

She ignores me. "You do realize that I can get a rental car, right? I'm perfectly capable of driving us back to L.A., so you can get away from McCrae right here and right now."

"You don't have to do that." Then, I pause. Despite what Heidi has said about wanting to take this trip with me, maybe she's ready to go home. "Do you want to go back right now?"

She takes her hand off the door and holds it open for me. "I do phone sex, Kylie. My customers aren't going anywhere, and besides, I really do want to see my folks. But I'm offering to take *you* home. I don't want to see you hurt, and now, you've got me all worried."

We walk side by side through the muggy carport, and in the distance, I can hear Cal and Wyatt's voices as they load their luggage and guitars into the back of the Suburban. I stop Heidi when we're several feet away from the SUV, clamping my hand down on her wrist. "Don't." My voice is hushed and more pleading than I intend for it to be. "Don't worry. I *want* to do this."

She drags her hand through her long brown hair, exhaling. "I know you do, but for the first time since you told me what your plan is, I actually believe that you just might go through with it, that you're done with him."

What she's saying is so similar to what Wyatt said this morning that I feel a cold pain spread across the inside of my chest.

"I hate when you don't get enough sleep because you're *way* too emo."

She pushes her shoulders back. "I'm worried because you're drawing this out, and it's going to be hell to walk away. I'm worried because, in the end, you'll hurt so much worse."

She's right. I am prolonging my time with Wyatt. I'm savoring him, feeding my addiction until the very end. It's twisted and unhealthy, but it's also something that I need. I drop my hand away from her arm. "Heidi, I'm good."

Instead of arguing with me or giving me her typical "I'm right because my last name is Wright" line, she only blinks and nods. A dangerous moisture is building up at the corners of her blue eyes, and I have to look away from them.

"Let's go to Albuquerque then," she says.

*** 

After we grab breakfast at a restaurant Heidi swears she has to try because she saw it on the Food Network, we get on the interstate toward New Mexico. Cal drives this time, but instead of sitting in the back with me, Wyatt opts for the passenger seat to keep him company.

Thanks to all the pancakes she ate at breakfast and her lack of sleep, Heidi immediately passes out in the back of the SUV. I stretch out in the second row, placing my feet against the door, and slide my earbuds in. A moment after I put The Kills playlist on shuffle, the powerful beat of "Future Starts Slow" pumps into my eardrums. Closing my eyes, I softly hum along while tapping my fingers on my thighs in time with the rhythm.

I'm not sure when I fell asleep, but the next thing I know, Wyatt's touching my shoulder, shaking me awake. He's standing with the door opened wide, leaning back, as his eyes skim over me.

"Cal needed a Red Bull. You want anything?"

I blink up at him a few times until my dark brown eyes adjust to the light. Groaning, I shake my head and pull my earbuds out. "I'm good. I'm just going to go back to—"

He reaches into the car for my hand, brushing against my breast in the process. It's an innocent touch, but it's still enough to make me shiver. "It's a long drive, beautiful. Come out for a few minutes."

"There'll be another stop." I yawn, and then I realize that I don't hear Heidi's soft snoring from the backseat. I sit up and see that she's gone. If Heidi figured it was a good idea to get out of the Suburban for a break it must mean Cal's not planning on making another stop for several hours, so it's probably a good idea for me to get out too. "What time is it?"

"Noon."

Reaching around on the floor for my aviator sunglasses, I glimpse up at him and lift an eyebrow. "Cal couldn't even last two hours without having to stop?" Wyatt's lips quirk up, and I laugh as I scoot to the end of the bench seat. "God, maybe I should drive."

"We'll probably get there faster." Holding my knees between his legs, he slides his fingers down my forearm until they find my hand. I swallow hard as he lifts my fingers to his mouth, rubbing his lip ring along my knuckles.

"You shouldn't do that."

"Believe me, beautiful, I know. It's been hell not climbing back there with you after the shit you started this morning." He drops my hand and begins to help me out of the Suburban.

"How long are we stopping—" I start, but I'm unable to finish as I step around him. Instead of a convenience store, I'm facing the front door of a crappy motel room. I clench my fists, digging my nails into my palms so deep that pain shoots up my wrists, as I take a hesitant step forward. When I speak, my voice is strained. "Where are Heidi and Cal?"

Wyatt comes up beside me, and I feel the lines of his body press against my side. I stiffen and turn my face away from him a little. "Where are they?" I repeat.

"At the convenience store across the street. We need to talk." Despite my cold shoulder, he grabs my hand and leads me to the front of the Suburban. He leans against the grill, but I stand with my back straight, glaring at the door to the motel room as if it'll fly open at any second and slap me across my face.

In a way, it already has.

"Why would we stop here?" I demand. "Why would you want to talk *here*?"

"You remember this place?"

*How the hell could I forget?* This is the same motel where we first made love. It's the place where he found me after my four-month marriage to Brad came to an end. While I was asleep, our trip had taken a detour, and now, we're in Livingston.

"Do you remember?" he asks again.

I nod slowly, and each tiny movement of my head makes me feel like I'm going under. "I stayed in that room down there the first time." I point my finger to the left toward the room at the end of the row of identical doors. "And in this one the last time." I incline my head to the door in front of us, room number 32. It's sad that I still remember both rooms. "You play so fucking dirty."

"I told you I was going to remind you why you fell, Kylie."

My breath hitches. "By bringing me back here? Do you think it was worth adding extra time to your trip?"

"I have so much to say to you. It seemed like this would be the best place to do it."

"We've already said enough here."

He's quiet, and I know he's thinking about the room at the end of the row. He's thinking about how I told him everything about myself, how I showed him each tiny scar, five of them in all, and how I tried my best to explain why I did it. That same night, he told me how he aspired to be a better man than his father, a womanizing drunk who hadn't made it as a guitarist, who flaunted women in front of Wyatt's mother until she took off.

*"I didn't even mind him beating the shit out of me," Wyatt says, pulling me closer to him in the hotel bed. He inhales my scent, and it's Ralph Lauren's Romance.*

*He's quiet after that, and the only sound in the room is Chevelle's "The Red." He waits until the song is finished, and then he says, "But the way she left without even giving me a second thought…it still fucks me up, Kylie. She didn't give a shit about me."*

*"I'm so sorry." Tears are forming in my eyes because I feel selfish. I feel like the most selfish bitch in the world for complaining to him earlier about not meeting anyone's expectations and retaliating by punishing myself. I cried about disappointing my parents when his had let him down too many times.*

*He pulls away from me, cupping my chin. "Don't be sorry, beautiful. I've got you, don't I?"*

*"Yeah, you do."*

*His chest rises heavily, and he makes a noise that sounds nothing like Wyatt McCrae. This is the first time in all the years I've known him that I've seen him nervous, and it sends a wave of anxiety through me. I pull the sheets up to my chin. "Is everything okay?" I ask hesitantly.*

He snorts. "Yeah and fuck no. Lucas will fucking kill me for going here with you." I start to respond, but he shakes his head. "It'll be alright."

"Alright," I whisper despite the pain in my throat. Wyatt's right about Lucas, and it's impossible for me not to dart my gaze at the door as if my brother will barge in at any moment.

"Relax," Wyatt orders. He brings my hand up to his lips and turns it slightly to kiss my wrist. "I meant what I said in the car, Kylie. Don't ever hurt yourself again. You want to get rid of the pressure? You take it out on me. Hit me, scratch me, do whatever the fuck you want, but don't do that shit to yourself again."

"Alright, then don't lie to me," I counter, staring at him hard.

If he were honest about his home life before tonight, I wouldn't ask. Instead, he lied to me and to Lucas for years. He led us to believe that his relationship with his father was perfect, instead of a heartbreaking tangle of deteriorating knots. The man lying next to me has felt abandoned and beaten and unwanted. I refuse to let him feel any of those emotions again, especially after tonight.

"Then you've got to tell me the truth, too, beautiful."

*I nod. "No matter what we are after this tour ends, don't ever treat me like I'm fragile."*

*He nods. "I won't," he says. Before he closes the space between our mouths, he adds, "But I've never thought for one moment that you're fragile, Ky."*

Eight years later and judging by the strained, distant look on his face, he's thinking about all that. When his nostrils flare and his gaze darts to the door directly in front of us, my mind goes to our second time at this motel—when we talked about Brenna in room number 37.

"Fuck, I've taken you for granted, Ky," he whispers harshly.

I stare down at a crack in the asphalt. "Yeah, you have."

He reaches out to me, and maybe it's the effect of being back at this hotel, but I step toward him, closing my eyes when his rough fingertips knead into the nape of my neck. "This is the last time I'll try to remind you, Ky...if that's what you want." His forehead touches mine. "But, god, I had to show you."

"Show me what?"

"That when I think about the happiest times of my life, I think of this shithole right here."

*Me, too.* I dip my head, too afraid to try to manage words right now.

"I want you with me the rest of this trip. Sleeping in my bed. Waking up next to me. My girl, just this last time."

Like the memories of our past, I can almost clearly see our future—a future where we're not together, where other people will give us exactly what we've been looking for with each other.

And I loathe it.

I loathe it so goddamn much that I speak without thinking.

"I'll stay with you until we get back to L.A.," I whisper.

He lowers his lips to my temple, blowing strands of blue-and-black away from my face. "And if I'm what you want by the time we get back, if we can finally fix ourselves, what the fuck then?"

I can hear Cal and Heidi coming across the parking lot, arguing loudly about the original lead guitarist of some band, and I swallow hard. "I…I don't know." Once again, the words tumble out before I have an opportunity to consider them, and his face cracks into a smile.

*Damn it.*

He backs away, slow to take his hands away from me. "It's not what I wanted to hear, Ky," he says just before Heidi and Cal come within earshot. "But that's so much fucking better than hearing never."

# CHAPTER ELEVEN

Because of the detour and then the long dinner break we take six hours into the trip, we don't arrive in Albuquerque until close to two the next morning. Though I've tried several times, I haven't slept a wink since we left the crappy hotel in Livingston. That place brought out so many memories—both good and bad—and I'm still restless as we check into the hotel.

When Wyatt opens the door to our room, I brush past him and step inside, my eyes scanning around the place we'll be staying at for the next couple of days.

The room is beautifully decorated in shades of royal blue and turquoise, but it's small compared to the last hotel. There's a mini-fridge, a flat screen television on a massive cherry wood cabinet, and a matching dresser and nightstand. The bed itself takes up the majority of the room's limited amount of space.

As Wyatt adjusts the thermostat to freezing, I sprawl out on the king-size mattress and close my eyes in pleasure as the memory foam hugs the curves of my body. "I swear you're trying to freeze me."

"Are you fucking with me?" He snorts and cocks his head to the side. "It's unbearable in here right now."

From where I'm lying, I can easily see the current temperature on the thermostat, and seventy degrees is anything but unbearable. "Maybe I should go sleep with Heidi and Cal," I tease. He comes to stand at the edge of the bed, smirking. "At least then, I won't wake up shivering."

"You'll wake up shivering but not because of the AC," he says, dragging his T-shirt over his head. He tosses it to the far side of the room, and it hits the balcony door.

He's about to climb onto the bed with me, but then his cell phone vibrates. Releasing an irritated sigh, he takes it out of his pocket. As he studies the message, pacing the narrow space between the end of the bed and the dresser, I prop myself up on my elbows.

After several seconds of silence, I blurt out exactly what I'm thinking. "Who's that?" I shouldn't ask—*god, I know I shouldn't ask*—but curiosity will keep me awake all night for all the wrong reasons. "Well?"

Digging his fingertips into his short blond hair, he shrugs. "Terra." He places his phone on the TV stand without replying to Hazard Anthem's gorgeous manager.

"Terra," I repeat, only it sounds like *terror*. I lie back down and whip the edge of the neatly tucked comforter over myself, but it only covers half my body. "She knows it's ridiculously late…or fuck, early, right?"

Wyatt yanks the blanket off me and joins me on the bed. He straddles my hips, and I stare up at him, keeping my gaze neutral. It's hard, considering he's moving his fingertip up and down the top of my thigh.

"She's having a party at her place and wants us to come by," he explains. "Nate's there." I don't miss the vicious way he says the front man's name.

I know that Wyatt has been to Albuquerque recently. I don't know the reason why because, technically, it's none of my business since he and I have never officially been a couple. I know I shouldn't ask him what he came here for, but now that I know Terra has a place in this city, only one thought is rolling through my head.

"Have you fucked her?" I demand.

"Are you serious, Kylie?"

I scoot up and slide my back against the headboard. This just causes him to move closer to me. He keeps his face level with mine, so I can smell the Mentos he chewed while we checked in. I touch his chin. He didn't shave this morning, and it's obvious.

"Have you and Terra ever had sex?" Each word is forced out, like seven single-worded questions.

If there's one thing I can say about Wyatt, it's that ever since I asked him never to lie to me eight years ago, he's been honest with me—heartbreakingly truthful at that. His blue eyes are hard as he shakes his head from side to side. "No."

Bowing my head briefly, I'm relieved that I'm sitting down, so he can't see how wobbly my knees are. *How would I have reacted if he told me that they have been together? What would I have said? Would I have walked out if he said yes?*

"Sorry I asked," I reply. When he strokes the right side of my face, I tilt my head slightly, welcoming his touch, moaning as his fingertips brush over the sensitive spot behind my ear.

"Terra's just with the band, Ky. After we're done here, you'll never have to see her again."

In this business, there's a slim chance of that happening, especially if Hazard Anthem goes mainstream. As long as I work for my brother, there's pretty much no chance in hell I'll be able to avoid Terra in the future. I narrow my eyes at Wyatt. "Why are you telling me this?"

He releases a rough sound, dragging his large hands over the strong features of his face. "Because you looked like you wanted to choke the shit out of her when you said her name."

Based on the way he reacted last night, if Nate—or any other man—texted me well after midnight, he'd wear the exact same look. Still, I suck my cheeks in, and I deny that crap. "I don't know Terra well enough to want to choke her, babe."

Wyatt's eyes challenge mine, but I glare back until he rises from the bed. "If you say so." When my eyebrows crease together, he takes my hands in his, pulling me roughly to my feet. "Come on. Shower."

As I search through my bag for body wash, he claims to have left one of his bags inside the Suburban. When he returns five minutes later, I'm already standing beneath the showerhead, washing my hair and softly humming "Crazy on You." He sets something on the outside of the tub before stripping down.

"Find what you were looking for?" I ask when he parts the curtain. I glance around him to see what he brought into the bathroom, but he jerks the fabric closed, his blue eyes dancing with amusement and desire.

"Looks like I have." Pressing his hands into the small of my back, he yanks me flush against his naked body. "Fuck, you're gorgeous, Ky." He lowers his mouth to my nipple, tugging it between his straight teeth, gently at first and then a little harder.

"My boobs weren't in the Suburban," I point out between gasps. Dragging my hands across his chest, I squeeze one of his nipples and then the other. He curses in surprise and catches my hands, linking our fingers.

"Smartass." He kisses my fingers before releasing them. "Close your eyes."

Sinking my teeth into my bottom lip, I shake my head. "Absolutely not, not until you—"

He spins me around, so I'm facing away from the showerhead. He covers my eyes with his hand. "Can you just listen for once?"

Pressing his body up against my back, he traces his tongue along each of my shoulder blades, sending all my senses into a chaotic frenzy, before kissing the spot in between. My muscles go taut as his mouth continues to move against my damp skin.

"I wouldn't be nearly as fun if I followed orders," I say despite my shallow breathing.

"So fucking true." Lowering his fingers from my eyes for a second, he leans over to grab whatever it is on the other side of the tub. He's back behind me, blindfolding me with his hand, before I can sneak a quick glimpse.

The surprise angle is getting really annoying, really fast. "So, why are we—" And then, I feel something new, something startlingly frigid. It's being held between his fingers against the folds of my sex, and I cry out. When I start to shiver away from the chill, he uncovers my brown eyes, moving his hand down to cup my breast.

"Ice?" I gasp.

As if to answer me, he traces the cube around my clit, grazing it back and forth until all that's left are his fingers stroking my center. He builds me up quickly, and I begin to shudder.

And then, suddenly, he stops. "Not yet, beautiful."

"Dick," I say between clenched teeth.

He slaps my ass and then flings aside the shower curtain. He dips his fingers inside the metal bucket full of ice. When he stands upright, I glance back over my shoulder, letting my eyes fall to his palm and the two cubes he's holding.

"Remember that night in Ohio a couple years ago?" he demands.

"Thought you said no more reminding me of the past."

"You want me to stop?" he whispers into my ear. Hesitantly, I shake my head. "Didn't think so."

He reaches around me, slicking the cubes over my breasts until my nipples tighten, and I realize that this is incredibly different from the night we spent in Ohio after a show several months ago. It was directly following one of our reconciliations a few weeks after blackbird tattoo number sixteen. Once the argument about his latest one-night stand was over, the lovemaking began, and we quickly forgot about the ice. By the time we fell asleep, it was nothing more than a bucketful of water.

Tonight, on the other hand, he seems to have the intention to use every single piece on my body. As if he guesses my thoughts, he glides a piece down my spine and stops at the small of my back, letting the remaining coolness trickle down. I suck a breath in through my teeth.

"I want to see the look on your face, Ky."

Another piece of ice slides between my thighs. This time, he holds it against my center until I reach both hands behind me, searching for anything to hold on to. One hand finds his hip while the other grips his dick, feeling it strain against my palm.

"Fuck," he says in a low voice. "Turn around."

I know what he's about to do the second he grabs a small handful from within the ice pail. He begins to kneel down in front of me, but I stop him and bring his hand to my mouth. Keeping my chocolate brown eyes glued to his, I wrap my lips around the ice, my fingers clenching on to his wrists as I slide each piece inside my mouth.

Before he can stop me and before the frigid sensation is gone, I skim down the length of his slick body until my knees touch the warm shower floor. As soon as I take his cock into my mouth, gripping his hips hard as I adjust to his size combined with the ice cubes, he cups the sides of my face, gazing down at me.

"God, Kylie," he groans as I move my mouth faster, harder around his cock.

Once the ice melts away, I grab more, but my lips never break contact with his body. I touch the ice directly to his erection, and he makes a noise in the back of his throat as I trace cold circles around him.

Finally, his hands knot into my hair. "This is dangerous," he warns.

I glide my tongue over all the spots where the ice has just melted, and then I lean back, staring up at him. His blue eyes are soft with desire and fatigue.

"I want it to be dangerous," I whisper before lowering my lips.

He holds my face between his hands, massaging my temples, as my mouth explores him while my fingers continue to dig into his hips. He moans when I encircle my hands around the base of his cock, pushing and pulling him to me, and when he releases, he says my name. He's still saying it as he pulls me to my feet.

He wraps my legs around his toned waist and pins me roughly to the shower wall. "Let me touch you, beautiful."

I clutch on to his shoulders, nodding. "God, I need you to."

He pushes his fingers between my slick folds, thrusting two in and out of me. As he moves his hand in a quick tempo, his palm teases my clit until I climax.

Even then, he's left me begging for more. "I want all of you," I whisper frantically against his mouth. "I fucking need you."

He doesn't say a word as he carries me into the other room to the king-size bed, our bodies still dripping wet from the shower, but his eyes tell me exactly what I want to know.

He needs me just as much.

\*\*\*

A few hours later, we're still awake as the first glimpse of the Albuquerque sunlight creeps into our room. The side of my face is pressed against his chest, and I listen to him quietly hum something that sounds like an off-key Chevelle-inspired medley featuring "Send the Pain Below" and "Wonder What's Next." He adds in words every once in a while I rub my thumb and forefinger in gentle circles over the *All Does Not End Well* tattoo on his neck.

Sleepy laughter bubbles from my chest as I prop myself up on my elbow. "You're the worst singer I've ever fucking heard."

"The worst?" He shoots me a look of disbelief. "I'm sure you've heard worse."

I shake my head slowly. He caresses my shoulder and the curve of my ass, causing a delicious tingle to spread through my body, as he guides me on top of him.

"Sorry, McCrae," I say. I move my hips against him, and he slides his fingers from my shoulder down to my side, so he can grip my ass with both hands. "Stick to using your hands."

He doesn't respond. Instead, he sucks on the tip of his thumb before pressing it to my clit, and then I'm blissfully lost.

\*\*\*

As much as my body and brain is desperate for some rest, I get very little. Heidi surprises me by showing up at my room at 9:47 a.m. She's dressed for the day and wearing a satisfied grin that can only come from one thing—sleep.

"Where's Wyatt?" she questions, trying to peek inside my room.

I ease the door closed until nothing more than a tiny sliver of light is between us. She narrows her eyes but doesn't try to sneak another glance.

"You look...perky today." And I'm not talking about her bright pink top or her even brighter pink lipstick. This is the most well-rested I've seen Heidi since we met up in New Orleans a week ago.

Apparently, rooming with Cal is good for her.

"Sleep is your friend," she says.

I roll my eyes up toward the ceiling. "Thanks for the pointer, *Lucas*."

"I'm going out for breakfast," she announces. When I give her a blatantly unexpressive look, she clenches her teeth into a pleading smile. "You're hungry, right?"

Actually, I'm starving, but I'm tired, too. I spent fourteen hours inside of the Suburban yesterday. Not to mention, most of the night was spent with Wyatt inside me. I should sleep. I should turn her down and take my ass right back to that amazing memory foam mattress and the naked man currently lying on it.

But then my stomach makes a noise, and Heidi nods her head slowly, her brown waves swooshing back and forth over her face. "There's a place next door. Just go throw on some pants, and we can walk over."

Groaning, I glance down at the Motionless In White band tee I threw on just before I answered the door. I'm braless *and* pantyless, and there's no way I'm leaving my room without a shower. "Give me twenty, okay?"

"Any longer and I'll leave your ass," she warns as she heads toward the elevator.

I don't buy that for a second. I take as many shortcuts as possible to get dressed, including a shower that's so quick I'm not sure the pipes had time to heat up to their full potential. As I drag another band tee over my head—the colorful Three Days Grace shirt that's by far one of my favorites—Wyatt wakes up.

He sits up in bed and watches me intensely, his vivid blue eyes following my every movement. As I adjust my thong, he releases a string of curse words. "Get back in bed, Kylie."

I give him a pointed look and shake my head. "You'd think you've never watched a woman get dressed." The instant the words tumble from my lips, I regret them. Wyatt has watched plenty of women, including myself, get dressed. Dropping my gaze to the carpet, I run my tongue over my lips. "I've got to say, you're freaking me out with all the staring, McCrae."

"Because I want to wrap that fucking thong around your wrists and keep you here with me."

Despite the harshness of his words, his voice is tender, and I'm a little shaky as I squat down to poke my legs into a pair of ripped-up jeans. As I stand and button them, pleased that this pair actually fits without cutting into my girlie parts, I slide my bare feet into a pair of pink Chuck Taylors.

"Where are you headed?" he asks.

"Breakfast with Heidi."

He makes a sleepy noise and stretches his arms over his head. The sheets pool around his waist, dropping to show off his tan, muscular V. "I want *you* for breakfast."

My mouth goes dry because I want him too, but I turn away from him as I gather my hair into a short ponytail on top of my head. I've composed myself by the time I face him again. Leaning my butt against the cherry wood TV stand, I cock my head to the side. "You'll be here when I come back?" There's a hopeful edge to my voice, but what's surprising is the way the question comes out so easily. Then, I realize that for the first time, this screwed-up thing between us seems like a real relationship.

"No." He shakes his head, and his full lips draw down into a frown. "Setting up with Hazard Anthem and running through the set. Then, I've got a few more things to take care of. Won't be back until right before it's time to get you tonight."

I try not to think about if Terra will be there, considering her late-night party invitation. "Okay, well, I'll text you if I need anything," I say. When he cocks an eyebrow suggestively, I groan. "That's all you think about."

"Your ass is too good not to."

I'm still feeling the effect of his words as I sprint down the stairs to the lobby.

Once Heidi sees me, she pops up from her chair and meets me halfway. "What took you so long?" She looks me up and down, examining everything from my clothes to my messy hairstyle, before she cocks an eyebrow.

"What the hell is wrong with me?" I ask breathlessly. When she shrugs, I release a frustrated moan. "It's Wyatt. He touches me or talks to me, and I'm a total wreck."

"Yikes, I thought we weren't supposed to touch the subject of Wyatt touching you with a giant pole," she reminds me, her voice lowered to a whisper. As we take the revolving door to the outside of the hotel, she glances over to me. "Something's happened since yesterday morning."

"I'm batshit insane."

"He wants a second chance?" She points her finger to the right toward the restaurant next door. As we walk across the hotel parking lot, she asks another question before I have the chance to answer the first. "And you're seriously thinking about it?" Heidi's soft voice is full of amazement.

I slide my hands up the front of my jeans, wiping off the perspiration from my palms. "He doesn't want to give me up."

"Because he's not stupid, Kylie," she says as I hold open the restaurant door for her. She dashes inside and then smiles at the hostess, holding up two fingers. Lowering her voice as we follow the woman to our table, Heidi says, "He'll fight for you, but if you decide you don't want to be with him, what then?"

I wait until we're alone to answer her. "If I'm happy, he won't pursue me."

Her pink lips press into a thin line, and I know she's calling bullshit. "Did he tell you that?" When I nod, she shakes her head. "Do you think that'll actually happen? He's addicted to you."

Our waiter, a skinny guy with tattooed wrists peeking out from his long-sleeved button-up, stops by our table to take our order. I point to a random spot on the menu that turns out to be the western omelet. I barely even notice the way the waiter's eyes scan over me as he takes our menus and promises to return shortly with our drinks.

Heidi sighs. "And you're obviously too addicted to him to notice anyone else."

I trace back and forth over the corner of the napkin wrapped around the silverware, my finger skimming the prongs of the fork. There's no point in denying what she has just pointed out now and so many other times before. I'm addicted to Wyatt on so many levels that it's apparent to anyone who sees us together and who knows what we're like apart.

We hurt each other.

Then, we mend ourselves.

And then, we do it all over again, only more violently.

Wyatt and I are our worst enablers. We always have been. If I didn't go to New Orleans, I probably would have been fine. If I had gone to him instead, this wouldn't be a conflict.

But I didn't go to him. I didn't meet him halfway.

He came to me—something he's only done a handful of times since we had started this twisted thing.

Our waiter returns to the table, and a dimpled grin slides easily over his features as he sets my orange juice down in front of me. "Need anything else?" he asks.

Heidi covers her mouth and coughs.

I ignore her. "Thanks, but I'm good."

He asks Heidi the same but with a little less enthusiasm, and when he leaves, she eye-humps him until he turns the corner. "I swear, Kylie, you're like sex on a—"

Chevelle blasts loudly from the inside of my pocket. I scramble to grab my phone as several people around us turn in our direction, their eyebrows gathering together at the noise. Pressing my thumb to the button on the side of the iPhone, I manage to silence it. I flip the phone over and wrinkle up my nose when I see *Unknown* flash on the screen.

"It might be Officer Townsend calling about our stuff." I stand up, and Heidi bobs her head enthusiastically as if she truly believes that all our belongings have been recovered and aren't currently in a New Orleans pawnshop. "Be right back," I promise, leaving her at our table.

I accept the call, but I wait until I dart out of the front double doors to say hello.

"I'm trying to reach Lucas Wolfe," a crisp female voice says.

If someone is calling this number for my brother, it's no doubt a business call. I turn on my professional voice, smiling widely to sound more pleasant. "This is his assistant, Kylie. I'd be more than happy to help you." As I pace back and forth in front of the bench that's beside the cigarette receptacle, I hear the sound of the woman's fingers rapidly flying over a keyboard. A moment later, she asks me to verify the last four digits of both my and Lucas's social security numbers. Once I do so, she tells me who she is—a representative from his business banking account.

And then, she delivers news that I just know is going to bite me in the ass.

"Due to the most recent transaction, Mr. Wolfe's checking account is currently overdrawn by $1,347. Would you like to transfer money from one of his other accounts to cover the overdraft?"

# CHAPTER TWELVE

"It's going to be alright," Heidi reassures me twenty minutes later as

we hurry through the door of the room she and Cal are sharing. She's

been telling me the same thing since I sat back down for breakfast.

Each time, she gives me her soothing voice that I'm sure she uses on

her phone sex customers. Still, I only managed to down half of my

western omelet before my stomach pitched violently.

All I can think about is how Lucas will react once I break

the news to him that Shiner Bock had somehow managed to break

into his bank account before I canceled my cards.

"Kylie, I swear it's fine." Heidi puts the small handbag she

bought in the hotel's gift shop into a compartment in the closet.

I sit down on the floor by the mini-fridge and start pulling

up the bank's website on my iPhone. "He's going to flip the fuck

out."

She kneels down in front of me, taking my chin in her

hands. "Relax. Banks fix this kind of thing all the time. Especially since you've got a police report. Just take a deep breath and get it figured out."

I start to nod, but then my phone beeps three times. I drop my gaze, letting out a curse when I see the low battery indicator flashing across the screen. "Do you have a charger I can use?"

"I think Cal does." I watch as she goes to the queen bed on the right side of the room. She glances around until she finally spots what she's searching for on the side closest to the wall. As she brings me Cal's phone charger, I realize that both beds look like they've been slept in.

When I'm not freaking out about my job, I'll mention that to her.

Plugging my phone into the wall outlet, I log in to Lucas's bank account, using the username and password he set up for me a few years ago. Almost immediately, I receive an error message— *Incorrect Username or Password.*

"Calm down," I tell myself although my voice sounds anything but cool and collected. The last thing I want is to fumble with the keyboard so many times that I'm locked out for the next twenty-four hours.

"Yes, keep calm, babe," Heidi says as she fishes a cigarette out of her luggage.

She hasn't smoked in days, and I feel bad for stressing her out to the point where she needs to temporarily pick up the habit again.

As she darts out the balcony door to smoke, I try to get into the account again, typing each letter and number slowly. Once more, I'm denied access. "Shit."

I close the Internet and open the Notes app, sorting through rows of reminders until I find the one I'm looking for—Lucas's personal login. After I commit the details to my memory, I retry logging in to the bank account.

"Thank God," I whisper when I'm not kicked out.

A few different accounts are listed on this page, and I click on the one the bank representative mentioned when I talked to her. I scroll through and study the recent transactions, and I feel absolutely sick to my stomach.

Several recent transfers have come into this particular account, each one from Lucas's accounts at other banks, equaling more than $200,000 in all. At the top of the screen under pending transactions, there are two purchases—one for the flight I secured for him the other day and the other for an outbound wire transfer in the amount of $250,000.

It's a ridiculously insane amount of money.

And deep down, I know this is something that Shiner Bock definitely has nothing to do with.

Money like this has Samantha Wolfe written all over it.

"Heidi," I call out.

She peeks her head back inside the room. "Yeah?"

"I'm going to go back to my room to call Lucas, okay?"

"Are you sure you're ready to talk to him?" Frowning, she steps inside. Her cigarette is still in her hand, and even though it's one of my vices too, I cough when the smoke curls around my face. "Sorry," she says, stretching the offending hand out the door as she waits for me to respond.

Gripping the mini-fridge, I pull myself up to my feet. "I'm sure I'm ready." Just to reassure her, I muster a confident smile. "I think I figured things out, and we'll probably be able to fix it fast."

She releases a deep breath. "Thank God."

***

As I take the stairs back to my room, I try to call Lucas. I'm not

surprised when I'm redirected to his voice mail. Over the next hour,

while anxiously watching a horror movie on HBO, I attempt to get in

touch with my brother three additional times. I'm debating on

whether or not I should call the one person Lucas will answer for—

our mom—when my phone rings, and I see his name on the screen.

He doesn't say hello. He doesn't say anything, and I take it

upon myself to initiate the conversation.

"Lucas," I say, trying to keep my voice calm, "why is there a

huge chunk of money missing out of your business account?"

A quarter of a million dollars isn't just a huge chunk of

money though. It's several years of my income, and it's gone from an

account that I'm supposed to be monitoring.

The man who answers me a few seconds later doesn't sound

like my older brother at all. He sounds broken, like a wounded

animal. "It's nothing. Mind your own fucking business, Kylie."

The fear that has seized my chest for the last hour and a half

suddenly shifts, and now, it feels like poison rippling through my body, wrapping around my bones, and slithering through my veins. "Not on your life, Lucas. It's Sam, isn't it? Are you paying that bitch off again? Where's Sienna? What the—"

When I hear the faint click, I know that I've lost him. I know that whatever it is my brother's gotten himself involved with has only gotten worse since he and Sienna took off for Atlanta.

I feel like I'm dying inside from worry.

For several minutes, I sit silently on the bed, inhaling the faint masculine scent Wyatt left behind. I know what I have to do. I know that I have to call Sienna to find out what she knows about my brother, but I also know that I'm not going to like what I hear. I know that there's a 99.9 percent chance she's been burned by all of this.

By the time I work up the nerve to call her, I'm crying.

"Please tell me he didn't?" More than ever before, I want to be wrong. I want her to tell me that she's still with Lucas, and he hasn't kicked her out.

But I'm not wrong.

Her voice sounds like she's a million miles away as she answers me, "Why does it matter?"

It matters because I wanted my brother to take care of her. I want him to be happy. It matters because I was the one who convinced her to go along with him. I was the one who told her that taking Lucas up on his offer would be all worth it.

But judging by the way Sienna sounds today, I was wrong about all of that.

"He's letting her control him," I explain. "I checked his…" I pause and take a deep breath, squeezing my eyes tight in hopes that it will keep me from picturing Samantha's fucked-up sneer. "He sent her a wire this morning for two hundred and fifty grand, and then I called him."

There's more silence on Sienna's end of the line. I climb out of the bed, barely feeling the thick carpet beneath my feet as I pace the short width of the hotel room. I try not to imagine what he could have said to Sienna before he made her leave him. I try not to think about what she must think of me right now for convincing her to be with him.

But it's impossible for me not to think about these things.

Finally, the sound of nothing but heavy breathing does me in, and I lean against the dresser, gripping the edges of the wood.

"She's got something on him, Sienna. I've got no fucking clue what it is, but she threatened him. She doesn't want him to be happy. She's—"

Sienna makes a soft noise, a sound of acknowledgment. "Kylie, I'll call you back."

"Let me talk to him. Let me figure out why she's screwing him over, and I can fix—"

Then, I realize that she's ended the conversation, and I'm making promises to nobody other than myself. Even though I desperately want to, I don't call her back because it won't help either of us right now. Hearing my voice again so soon will only make her hurt more. So, I call the source behind all of her pain.

He doesn't answer my call, and I start to leave a message. More than anything, I want to let Lucas know exactly how I feel about him at this very moment, but then I realize that it won't do me any good. If he responds, it will only be in defense. He'll only remind me of just how messed up my own relationship with Wyatt is. I end the call and clench the iPhone as tightly as possible to resist the urge to hurl it across the room.

As I ease down onto the edge of the bed with my face buried in my hands, I'm not sure if I'm crying more for Sienna and my brother or for myself and Wyatt McCrae.

***

For the remainder of the day, I put on the most believable facade possible. Heidi and I explore Albuquerque since this is her first visit here, and she ropes me into doing everything from shopping to trying to get past the ID verification at a casino she's read good reviews about. It doesn't work, and we're turned away.

As we take a taxi back to our hotel to get dressed for tonight's show, she finally brings up Lucas. I tiptoe around the topic for several questions until she asks, "So, I'm guessing you got everything worked out for him."

I tighten my hands into fists in my lap, giving Heidi a nod. "Wrapped up neatly and tied with a bow." *An incredibly sad and frayed bow that will unravel into a million pieces at any moment.*

"Thank God. I'd feel like shit if Finn messed something up for Lucas."

A tiny smile crosses my lips. "*Finn* would feel like shit if he screwed with Lucas." Saying that only makes my thoughts ping back to Samantha.

My brother is hotheaded, moody, and commanding. He's the first to start a fight and the last to say sorry. *So, why the fuck is he pouring his money into Samantha's hands the moment she snaps her claws?*

After the taxi driver drops us off at the hotel, I attempt to think about anything but Sam and Lucas and Sienna. Of course, the second Wyatt comes back to the room, striding across the floor with his hands pushed deep into his pockets, he blows that to hell.

He stands behind me as I apply my makeup in the bathroom mirror. "Something's wrong, Ky." The alarm is back in his voice. It's the same panic that was present back in New Orleans on the night Shiner Bock ransacked my room.

I look up, glancing at his reflection and mine. "Had a fight with Lucas."

"He say something fucked-up to you?" he demands, leaning his muscular long body up against the door frame.

I shake my head. Regardless of how angry I am with my brother, there's only so much of his personal life I want to put out there, not even to Wyatt, who's Lucas's best friend. "He hurt Sienna."

Wyatt mouths her name a couple times before recognition dawns in his blue eyes. "And she came after you for that?"

"No. That's just it. She didn't say *anything*."

I carefully apply my lipstick, an electric blue I found at Sephora that matches the blue in my hair, before I turn to face him. His gaze slides up my body from the blue patent stilettos to the leather-looking leggings and finally to the asymmetrical black top that brings out every positive aspect of my figure. His eyes are appreciative and hungry, making my eyes drop to the tile floor.

"Don't look at me like that when I'm angry."

He crooks his finger, beckoning me to him. Tentatively, I step forward until his strong hands circle around me, clasping on to the sides of my bottom. "You're not angry at me, beautiful." He backs me up against the door frame. "Are you?"

Thoughts of how I cried over him earlier this afternoon force their way into my head. I jab my tongue into my cheek. "I'm trying not to be."

Burying his face into my hair, he slides his palms up and down my hips. "Then, don't be. Deal with your brother's shit tomorrow. Be mine tonight."

Arching my back, I lean away from him and slip my fingers into his hair, tugging hard. His eyes watch mine for what seems like hours before he bends his head to press tiny kisses all over my face and neck and chest, ruffling the flimsy fabric of my shirt.

"Deal with Lucas tomorrow," he says again in a more forceful voice. "You're mine tonight."

I don't correct him and let him know that tomorrow is Saturday, the last show before we go back to L.A. It could potentially be the last show of our relationship if we choose to go our separate ways.

"No," I tell him, "you're mine."

# CHAPTER THIRTEEN

The Twisted Keg, the bar where the band is playing, is located in downtown Albuquerque. It's twice the size of the bar in Houston, and there are at least three times as many people inside. After Wyatt smooths things over with security at the door, I'm allowed entry without my ID. He kisses me longingly before disappearing to join the band, and I find myself wanting to go with him.

"Thought you guys weren't into PDA," Heidi says loudly from behind me as we squeeze through the crowd of tightly packed bodies.

"We're not." I shoot a glance over my shoulder to find her grinning. Turning my gaze back to the crowd in front of us for a moment, I ask, "Why do I feel like this is a screwed up riot just waiting to happen?"

She sucks in a breath, and I glance back to see her making a face at a woman who's a few feet away from us. Judging by the way she's moving her foot, I can only assume Heidi's toe has fallen victim to the other woman's lethal-looking stilettos. "Because you've been to these types of things enough times to know how quickly crap can get crazy."

I scan the crowd, playing Where Are the Bouncers?, and I quickly come to terms with the fact that there's little security. I shift uncomfortably, watching the stage as the band is introduced. "Let's hope this isn't one of the crazy ones." Still, I suddenly wish I didn't wear such impractical shoes.

Fanning her flushed face, Heidi nods her head toward the teeming bar, and I groan. "It's a mob. Do you really want a drink that bad?"

"Would you prefer to sit around thirsty all night? Besides, I hate to say this, but you look like you need a beer or two."

*Good point.* After all the drama from earlier today, battling a mob of bargoers to get a drink doesn't seem so bad. As we push our way through the crowd, the band starts the first song of their set. It's a cover that I know better than the back of my hand, and when I start to hum along with it, amusement flickers in Heidi's cornflower blue eyes.

"You think Lucas would shit a brick if he knew Hazard Anthem is playing 'All Over You'?"

Because I don't want thoughts of my brother and his overall stupidity to screw with my night, I shrug. "He shouldn't be. It's a compliment."

Focusing her eyes on the stage, she cocks her head to the side. "Nate's almost as good as him."

"Nowhere near it, babe."

There's still a line for drinks when we finally push our way up to the bar, but luckily, it only takes a couple minutes before one of the bartenders—a woman wearing a vintage polka dot halter that I have in my closet—takes our order. "What can I do you for, ladies?" Her scarlet-painted lips drag up into a smile.

Heidi twists her mouth like she's trying to decide, but of course, she already knows what she wants. If she doesn't order beer, she always springs for a 7-and-7. Tonight is no different, and since we're staying inside of our comfort zone, I ask for a bloody mary, triple shot.

The barmaid's penciled-in eyebrows jerk up. "In the mood to fuck something up?" She supports her elbows on the bar counter, staring back and forth between Heidi and me.

"Nah," I say. "I just like my vodka."

She leans back, shaking her head and laughing. "Yeah, me, too. I'll make you a double, hon." She gives me a look that screams I should have known better than to ask for more.

As soon as we have our drinks in hand, Heidi leaves the barmaid an incredibly generous tip, and then my best friend looks at me, mouthing something. It takes me a few tries, but I finally make out what she's yelling over the deafening sound of voices and music. "Let's move closer!"

We squeeze through the mass congregating around the stage, and I grit my teeth when someone jostles into me, causing me to spill a few drops of my drink on myself. *Great, now I'll smell like Betsey Johnson perfume, cigarette smoke, and Tabasco sauce for the rest of the night.*

Heidi and I don't stop moving until we're near the front of the fray, jammed between a few people wearing T-shirts from Your Toxic Sequel's last tour. Once the tall guy standing in front of me moves out of the way, my brown eyes instantly locate Wyatt. He doesn't see me, but every few moments, his eyes flick around the crowd.

Cal manages to spot us though, and he gives us a wink that I'm certain is meant for Heidi. She must also see it because she grins like the Cheshire Cat before tucking a lock of her curly hair behind her ear.

I lean in close to her. "You're disgustingly cute."

She rolls her eyes, holding her hand in front of her defensively. "Trust me, it's not even like that. He just likes to get a reaction out of me." Her cheeks are tinged with color, and I'm guessing Cal's getting exactly what he wants. Before I can say another word, she nods her head to the side of the stage. "There's Terra."

My gaze wanders over in the general direction, and I spot the blonde woman holding her phone up high, recording the show. She's with some man, and every few seconds, she glances up at him and says something. I work my lip between my teeth, trying desperately to remember where I've seen the guy before. When it doesn't come to me, I focus my attention on the music.

The band is halfway through a song they didn't play in Houston when I feel a hand touch my ass. It's not a brush or an innocent jab but a rough squeeze. Gripping my drink tightly, I count to three before I turn to face the guy who's feeling me up.

If I were into backwards-baseball-cap-wearing douche bags who've had too much to drink, I might consider him decent-looking enough. Since I'm not, I tilt my head to the side. "I don't like being touched," I say loud enough to be heard by several people around us.

He grins down at me. At first, he doesn't make a move to take his hand away, but then the guy with him says something in his ear. He shoots his buddy a sharp look as he drops his hand to his side.

"You're empty." He tries to take the clear plastic cup away from me, but I tighten my grip around it. "Hey, I just want to buy you a drink," he says defensively.

"Thanks, but I'm DD," I lie, lifting the corners of my mouth. "So, sorry." I glance over at Heidi who's already jerking her head in the opposite direction, her light blue eyes wary. I turn to follow her, but the guy grabs my wrist. When I confront him this time, I ditch the smile. Going about things the polite way with this asshole is getting me absolutely nowhere. "Get your hand off me."

"I'm trying to be nice to you."

I shoot a look at his friend and see his face is slowly turning red. "You should probably take him on home." To the drunken idiot, I jerk my arm away from his grip. It hurts like hell, but I keep the badass expression on my face. "You can be nice by fucking off."

Heidi practically wrenches me toward her, so we can get out of this situation, but when the guy grabs me again, I turn around and slam my fist into the first thing I can easily hit, his stomach. He doubles over, wheezing. As I open and close my hand by my side, I instantly regret punching him.

I should have kicked him in his balls.

"You fucking bitch," he growls.

His friend instantly steps in. "Dude, Dillon, leave her alone. She said—"

Dillon shrugs off the other man. He's about to say something to me, maybe even try to touch me again, but then two hands clasp on to his shoulders, spinning him around. I'm just now aware that the sound of the bass guitar is nowhere to be heard as I take in Wyatt standing inches away from me with all his features drawn into tight lines. I also realize how quiet the crowd seems despite the fact that the rest of the band is going on with the show.

"You want to put your hands on someone?" Wyatt asks Dillon, leaning close to him. "Try me, motherfucker."

Over his shoulder, I spot a big bear of a man stalking toward them. He's wearing a black T-shirt that has *Security* written in large bold print across the front of it.

"And I think I just wet myself," Heidi hisses into my ear, holding on to my forearm.

"Well?" Wyatt challenges again. When Dillon flips him the bird, I hold my breath, hoping McCrae's smart enough not to fly off the handle. Glancing at me for a second, he tells Dillon, "Yeah, fuck you, too."

My heart is beating so hard that I swear it's louder than Ben's drums. Wyatt starts toward me, wearing an apologetic smile, and because Heidi chooses that exact moment to say something right into my ear, I don't hear everything Dillon says next.

But I hear enough.

"Groupie slut."

I lose my breath for a moment just as Wyatt whirls on him. Dillon is lucky because the bouncer finally intervenes, wedging himself between them, breaking up what could have been a night in jail and a lawsuit for Wyatt.

"Show's over," Wyatt growls the moment he reaches my side. He pulls me to him, crushing my body against his.

I shake my head. "Absolutely not, McCrae."

The band finishes up the song they're currently playing, and Nate leans into the microphone, announcing that they're taking a fifteen-minute break before starting the next set.

Wyatt cocks an eyebrow mockingly. "Show's over for fifteen minutes then."

I feel multiple sets of eyes burning into us as Heidi and I follow close behind Wyatt to the bar manager's office. Cal and the Hazard Anthem boys are already inside the room.

Heidi plops down into the chair behind the giant U-shaped desk, exhaling and inhaling a few times. She glances around to each face, including mine. "Remind me why I go to bars again?"

"Well, that was fucking interesting," Ben comments, scratching the tip of one of his drumsticks against his shaved head.

He winks at me. "I think you could've taken that shithead down, but I can't say I wasn't happy to see McCrae jump off that stage."

Wyatt grins, but I can tell he's still angry. It's in his blue eyes and the way he keeps clenching and unclenching his fists. "A hundred bucks says the only thing Kylie was thinking about was bailing me out tonight."

I jerk my head from side to side, but it's mostly because I'm a shaky mess right now. "Please, I don't even have a debit card." When he rolls his eyes, I add, "But if you have to know, I was thinking of the lawsuits."

"You ever stop working?" Cal chimes in. I shake my head at him as he backs up toward the door. He makes a face and then glances toward the desk to my best friend. "Hey, Heidi?"

She leans forward. "Yes, douche bag?"

He grins. "You and me. Shots before we go back on?"

She's already on her feet, heading toward the door. She gazes back at me, widening her eyes like she still can't believe what just happened. *Hell, neither can I.* "You're buying. You know this, right?" she asks Cal.

"Please, I know how much money you make," he counters as he closes the door behind them.

Wyatt flicks his eyes between Nate and Ben until they take the hint to leave.

"Sorry about McCrae's stage dive," I say as they head to the door.

Nate waves it off. "Shit, he probably just got us a bunch of new fans with that move." He starts to say something else, but then he bites the corner of his lip and shakes his head. "Ten minutes left, fucker," he calls out to Wyatt as he and Ben exit the office.

Finally, I let my shoulders drop. When Wyatt leans back against the desk, I lay my head against his chest. "Lucas would've had your balls if you pulled a stunt like that on stage with YTS."

I feel him shrug. "There are more important things to me than music."

By the way he's looking down at me, like I'm the only thing he needs at this very moment, I believe him. "Careful saying things like that," I whisper.

He lifts my fingers to his lips. "But, god, it's true."

"Is it okay to come in?" a voice says from the door.

We slowly break apart and turn together to face Terra. She's leaning against the door frame, looking like a rock goddess in a black sequin tank top and dark skinny jeans. "The band's ready to go back on."

Wyatt dips his gaze back to mine, his blue eyes promising me that we'll continue later. "I'll see you after the show," he says before he sprints out of the manager's office.

For a few seconds, Terra's green eyes linger on his departing form before she turns to me. "So, that was interesting." Then, she blushes and shakes her head. "The, um…little conflict back there, I mean."

I cross my arms over my chest. "That's the same thing Ben said."

"I'm just glad you're alright."

She sounds like she genuinely cares that I'm safe, so I smile graciously at her. "Thanks."

"Do you want to head back out and listen to them? Or do you want to stick around in here? It's totally up to you."

"I'm good to watch. I'm so used to this kind of thing happening that I can almost predict how the night will end before the band starts playing."

"Shithead radar," she says as she walks out the door. "Nice."

We walk together toward the stage, and the crowd is so wrapped up in the band's current song that they seem to have moved on from the confrontation between Dillon, Wyatt, and me. I spot Heidi on the opposite side of the stage, close to where Cal is playing, and she waves me over. Before I can leave, Terra stops me.

"I know you couldn't make it out last night, but I'm having some after-show cocktails at my place."

She glances up at the stage, and though I don't follow her gaze, I know whom her eyes focus on. I struggle to keep my smile in place. It's all I can do to not say something negative, knowing it would damage Wyatt and Cal's relationship with Hazard Anthem.

"I hope you and the boys can make it out."

"We'll try," I promise before leaving her to join Heidi.

***

For the next forty-five minutes, I think of ways to avoid going to the after party without offending the rest of the band. When none come to mind, I decide that I can deal with Terra eye-humping Wyatt—at least for a few hours.

When the band's set is finished and they've loaded their equipment, Wyatt finds me in the crowd. He pulls me to him, looking at me like I'm the only person in the bar, even though Ben and Terra are only a few feet away from us.

"You know what I said about you being mine tonight?" he asks in a low voice. I nod. "That starts right fucking now."

# CHAPTER FOURTEEN

"Where are we going?" I demand as he pulls me toward the Suburban. It's located at the far end of the bar's parking lot, and I find myself glancing around cautiously to make sure Dillon's not waiting out here with a crowbar, wanting to start a fight with Wyatt. Fortunately, we make it to the SUV without running into trouble.

He presses the unlock button on the remote and opens the door for me. "You'll see when we get there."

I cross my arms over my chest, glancing at the entrance to the bar. "Should we at least tell Heidi and Cal?"

"You really think either of them care? Trust me, Ky, they're big kids. They can take care of themselves." He points to the leather passenger seat and gives me a wicked smile. "Now, get in."

He's quiet as we leave The Twisted Keg. He speeds past our hotel and the restaurant where Heidi and I ate this morning, continuing his silence.

As we exit the city limits of Albuquerque, my eyebrows shoot up. "I don't like surprises."

He tilts his head slightly, his blue eyes burning into me, as he grips the steering wheel with one hand. "But it's taking your mind off of Lucas's newest bullshit."

*Well, yes.* Tonight has been so hectic that I haven't had time to think about what's going on with my older brother. "So, you think that taking me to God knows where will keep me from reality?"

"Of course it will, Bluebird."

"It might help if you at least clue me in on where this escape is going to take place," I reply. He responds by lifting his shoulders, and I sit back in my seat, letting the sound of whatever's playing on Octane, my favorite Sirius station, fill the silence inside the Suburban.

I'm humming along to an Evans Blue song, staring out my window, when Wyatt drives past the *Welcome to Santa Fe* sign. Turning to look at him, I scoot as far as I can toward the center console and lean over so that my lips graze his ear. "Babe?"

His back straightens, and he glances at me from out of the corner of his eye. "Hmm?"

"Why the hell are we in Santa Fe?"

He twists his face to mine, leaving less than an inch between our mouths. As he accomplishes this, I'm amazed at how he manages to stay on the road. "Because I want to fuck you in every city I can before we go home in a couple days." When he laughs after he says this, I know he's screwing with me.

At least, I think he is.

I quickly find out what his plans are when he takes a series of turns. He finally swings the Suburban into a parking lot that's hardly large enough to fit the massive SUV. One corner of my mouth quirks up as I glance at the fluorescent lights on the building right in front of us.

"Piercings and tattoos," I say, and he grants me a nod. "So, which are you here for?" My eyes automatically dip down to his crotch, and I think of his Prince Albert.

He touches his right hand to the left side of his chest. "And before you ask…" He opens his door and gives me a cocky grin. "No, this isn't one that can wait until we get back to L.A."

"I wasn't going to ask," I say as I get out of the SUV. I join him at the front of the building where he slides his hand into my back pocket and stares down into my brown eyes. "It's late. You sure you want to do this tonight?"

"Corey's already expecting us. Best fucking artist I've ever met, beautiful, and he's only available right here."

He holds the door open for me. The second I step inside the tiny parlor, I'm immediately greeted by the aroma of green soap, fresh ink, and witch hazel. I inhale and exhale several times, letting the intoxicating familiar scent wash over me.

Wyatt lowers his mouth to my ear. "Does it to me, too, beautiful."

As I glide the tip of my tongue over my lips, he draws in a deep breath.

"Know what you're getting?" I ask.

He nods confidently just as a short man with surprisingly very little ink darts out from behind the curtain across the room. "Wyatt!"

Wyatt quickly introduces us. "Kylie, this is Corey. Corey, this is—"

"Bluebird," Corey says simply.

I swear I flush all the way down to the tips of my toes. *When did Wyatt tell this man about me? More importantly, what did he say?*

"Nice to meet you, too," I reply. I glance back and forth between them, hoping that Corey will tell me what Wyatt's said about me.

He doesn't, and while they talk, I wander to the lounge area and sit in a plush suede chair. Every few moments, I catch Corey or Wyatt glancing over in my direction, and it's unnerving. I pluck a giant binder from the coffee table and begin to flip through it, running my fingertips over each page of intricate tattoo designs.

After several minutes, from across the room, Corey asks me, "See anything you like?"

My lips curve into a smile as I nod my head. He's prepping the ink on his worktable, but he takes a moment to shoot me a curious look. "Too many. Your work is absolutely amazing."

Wyatt makes a little sound in the back of his throat that resembles a chuckle, drawing my attention to him. He's already in the chair with his shirt off, and his blue eyes rake over me.

"Want to watch?" Corey asks as he cleans Wyatt's skin.

I shake my head. For me, watching lost its novelty years ago, and besides, no artist wants somebody staring over his shoulder while he works. I reach for the next binder, and when I'm done with it, I pick up the next one. Once I'm out of photos to look at, I flip through the pages of *Inked* while listening to the soothing hum of the tattoo gun as Corey runs it across Wyatt's skin.

I'm on my fourth issue of the magazine, admiring a tattoo of a skull surrounded by orchids, when Wyatt finally calls me over. Glancing up, I realize that the sound of the machine has stopped.

Standing, I stretch out my legs, which have gone stiff from sitting so long. I cross the linoleum floor slowly, squinting at the design on the right side of his chest until I come right up on it. At the moment, it's just an outline. His skin is splotchy, but this is something I've seen before. It always heals.

What stops me from immediately saying anything is the design itself. It's a bird descending, and I study it carefully, starting from its tail feathers close to Wyatt's muscled left shoulder to its beak in the center of his chest. At first, I think it's a crow because of the creature's fierce features, but then I notice where the color is partially filled in along the wings.

And I realize that it's a bluebird.

An aggressive and powerful and utterly sexy bluebird.

Words finally find me. "It's gorgeous." I look up from the tattoo into Wyatt's eyes, feeling my throat swell at just how vulnerable they suddenly look. "It's my favorite."

And that's the truth. Out of every mark of ink on his body, this bird is the one that has the most significance to me. It's the one that I'll dream about.

Wyatt and I don't say too much to each other as he pays Corey, but when we get to the door to leave, I pause. "You okay, Ky?" he asks, touching my shoulder.

I grip the doorknob and shake my head. Turning around to face Corey, I clear my throat. He glances up from where he's cleaning his equipment and cocks an eyebrow. "Is it too late for you to do one for me?"

Corey's eyes dart from Wyatt to me, and he laughs. "If this motherfucker is paying, then hell no."

I draw my hand away from the doorknob to head over to speak to Corey about the design I'm looking for, but Wyatt stops me.

"It's not over yet," he says in a pained voice. "No more fucking blackbirds, Ky, not yet, not until you give me a chance."

I peel his fingers away from my arm, one by one, shivering when his thumb brushes the tiny scar on my wrist as he lets go. "No, no blackbirds."

It doesn't take Corey long to sanitize his work station, and once he's finished and I quietly tell him what I want, it takes him a total of fifteen minutes to draw up a sketch for me. Thirty-five minutes later, when the needle cuts into my finger like a razor blade, I suck in a deep breath of air. I can feel Wyatt's intense eyes on me from the other side of the room, but I keep my focus on watching Corey's boot work the foot pedal on the floor.

I go through the different emotions as Corey turns my skin into his canvas. At first, there's the pain. It builds up slowly until it feels like he's piercing everywhere at once. Then, there's the high, the sudden rush of adrenaline. It doesn't kick in until I'm numb to the needle, and the only thing I'm able to feel is the vibration from the tattoo gun. And last…there's the feeling of release. That doesn't come until Corey finally leans away from me, and I hold my hand in front of my face to examine the tattoo.

Gone is the name *Martin*, which has branded me for more than seven years. In its place is a knotted design. It races around my ring finger with a tiny bow in the center. My new ink is nowhere near as intricate as the bluebird between my shoulder blades, nowhere near as painful as the blackbirds on my collarbone, but it symbolizes something none of the others do.

*Letting go of the past.*

It's 2:49 a.m., when we climb back into the Suburban. Wyatt takes an alternate route out of Santa Fe, a back road, which causes the GPS to reset and estimate our time of arrival to 3:53 a.m.

He reaches into my lap and pulls my hand into his, being careful not to squeeze my wrapped-up finger. "I've been amazed by you since the first time I touched you, Ky. I've wanted every part of you since that day," he starts in a rough voice. "Do you know what the bluebird is for?"

"Happiness," I say, repeating what he explained to me about my own a few years ago. "A new beginning."

He shakes his head. "It's for you. You're my happiness, and I'll fight until the end to make sure you know that."

In all the years we've played this toxic game, in all the years when we've sworn off being a real couple, this is the closest he's come to telling me that he loves me. It's even closer than the time on my parents' porch four years ago, and it leaves me speechless.

I turn down the radio volume, canceling out the bittersweet grittiness of "By the Way," my favorite Theory of a Deadman song. I can't listen to a song about being ripped apart and saying good-bye to the one you love when Wyatt's sitting right next to me, telling me all these things.

"I can't let you go," he continues. "Not when you're the only goddamn thing on my mind. It's impossible."

I rub my hands back and forth over my face, letting his words seep in. He glances over at me, waiting, and I take a deep breath. "I can't promise you anything, but I know how I feel about you."

*I know that I'll hate it if he's with anyone else. I know that if I walk away from him without trying, I'll spend the rest of my life hating myself, regretting what could have been.*

*I know that despite it all, I love Wyatt too much for things to be as simple as a good-bye.*

I should have realized this all along.

"Come here," he growls.

"You're driving," I point out.

He's silent for a couple of minutes, but then he eases the Suburban down a narrow dirt road shrouded by pine trees. He cuts the ignition and the lights. "Come here." This time, his tone is far more demanding, and it makes my pulse race.

I crawl across the center console, and my breath catches when he jerks me into his lap. It's a tight fit, especially between the seat and the door, but I manage to place my legs on each side of his body.

"I can't be in the same room as you without wanting you close to me," he murmurs against my chin. He traces his lips down the column of my throat, the labret tickling my skin, and I shiver. "I can't even be in the same car without keeping my hands off you." His mouth touches the top of my left breast. He runs his tongue along it, and I arch my back until the steering wheel digs into my skin.

"We're probably in someone's driveway." Yet, I'm moaning and already moving my hips against his, heat pooling in the pit of my belly, as his cock grows hard beneath me.

"If I can't do anything without wanting you near me…" He reaches between my legs, ripping my leggings at the spot between my thighs. "Then, why the fuck do you think I'll ever stop trying?"

"You won't." I gasp when his fingers find my clit. He touches me through the outside of my panties, grinding the pad of his thumb against my sensitive flesh. "Unless I'm happy. If I were happy with someone else, something else, you'd stop wanting me."

He kisses me greedily, skimming his fingers inside my panties, as he digs his other hand into the small of my back. I move my hips in time with his every movement, sucking on his bottom lip after he's done the same to mine.

Finally, I grasp his cock through his jeans. "You'd stop wanting me then, wouldn't you?" I repeat what I said before he distracted me.

He drops his eyes to my hand on his dick. "Don't start shit you're not going to finish," he whispers. "But to answer your question, I'll never stop wanting you even if you are happy. I'd just know when to leave well enough alone."

His words make my head spin, and I drop my forehead to his shoulder. He continues to touch me as he whispers unintelligible things into my ear. I'm on the verge of climaxing when he pulls my hand away from the outside of his jeans. His fingers wrap around mine, and carefully, he helps me guide his zipper down.

"You're not going to come unless I'm fucking you," he says as I reach inside his boxers to stroke his cock. He touches me between my legs again, and I pull in a deep breath when I hear my panties rip apart between his strong fingers. "I want to feel everything, beautiful."

"I want you to fuck me," I whisper.

I lift my hips a little, so he can dig into his back pocket for the condom in his wallet. Once he's ready, he motions me forward. Gripping his shoulder with one hand, I guide his cock between my legs with the other, but he stops me before I can push him inside me.

He holds my hips tightly. "You're mine. No matter what you decide or who the fuck you end up with, you always will be."

"Is that right?" I tease.

A self-assured laugh comes from the back of his throat. "You'll always be mine."

"Show me."

Releasing a rough sound, he thrusts his cock deep inside me, and I dig my knees into the sides of his body. "I want to fuck you harder, Ky."

I cry out as he grasps my hips, rocking them fast and hard up his length and back down again. I hold on to his shoulders, not caring when pain streaks up my ring finger or when my back slams into the horn behind me. It beeps loudly, and it's the only sound other than our heavy breathing and the rhythm our bodies make with each other.

When I feel myself on the verge of an orgasm, I clench my pussy around him, and he buries his mouth into my shoulder. He murmurs something against the fabric of my black shirt as I come, and a moment later, he releases a groan, shuddering and driving himself into me until he reaches his climax.

As we catch our breath, I realize that he's right.

I am his.

# CHAPTER FIFTEEN

The sound of my phone ringing on the floor beside the bed wakes me up the following morning. I roll over to grab it, groaning when I see that it's another unknown caller. Even though I'm still livid with Lucas, I answer it immediately, almost expecting it to be his bank with another overdose of horrible news.

Instead, it's an officer from Louisiana, a female this time, calling with a status report on my case against Shiner Bock. I can't help but be impressed that someone is contacting me on a Saturday morning even if her call did drag me out of bed an hour earlier than I intended.

According to the officer, Finn and his grope-happy friend, James, have been caught. I let my shoulders slump forward in relief. "So, are they in custody?" I ask.

"As of yesterday afternoon, yes."

Even though I'm sure there's a slim chance in hell, I can't resist asking her whether or not any of my stuff was recovered.

"One moment, please," she says. I can hear her leafing through a stack of paperwork. Using the silence to my advantage, I mute my phone and dash into the bathroom to brush my teeth. I have a mouthful of toothpaste when she speaks again, surprising me. "Based on the report you filed, a few of your belongings were found on Finn Graham's person."

Rinsing out my mouth quickly, I take my phone off of mute. "Can you tell me what all you found of ours?"

"Unfortunately, I'm not allowed to give you details about the belongings Ms. Wright's reported missing due to our privacy policy, but I'd be happy to tell you which of your items were found."

"Thanks, that would be great."

I listen carefully as the officer reads through the list, which turns out to be a total of four things, about a quarter of my belongings that I reported stolen. The canceled credit cards and my driver's license were nowhere to be found, but I didn't exactly expect to get those back. I'm pretty sure they're all in a dumpster somewhere by now, and I make a mental note to put some type of alert on my credit report.

"Are you going to call Heidi? Or should I tell her to get in contact with you?" I ask as I wipe my mouth with a warm washcloth.

"We've already contacted Ms. Wright, and she's aware of the procedure to pick up her belongings."

I examine my smile in the mirror before I flip off the light switch and return to bed. "So, how exactly do we go about doing that?" I ask. "Is there any way I can get it shipped to my home address?"

"Do you have something to write with?"

"Just a second." Leaning over, I find the hotel's complimentary stationery set, which is just a stack of promotional sticky notes and a pen, inside the nightstand drawer. I grab a phone book and place one of the Post-its on it. "Okay, I'm ready."

As she speaks, I jot down a few things, but the gist of the whole recovery process is pretty simple. My belongings are in New Orleans, and they can't be mailed to me in California, meaning I'll have to physically go into their station with my ID—which I don't currently have—and sign a form. Since going back to Louisiana isn't in my plans for the near future, I ball up the note and toss it in the wastebasket as soon as the call ends. "Guess I won't be getting that crap back for a few months," I say under my breath.

"What crap?" Wyatt asks drowsily from beside me.

Placing the phone book back inside the nightstand drawer, I lean against the headboard and pull my knees to my chest. "The cops picked up the assholes who robbed my room."

"Assholes?" He stares at me incredulously. "I thought there was only one guy."

When I shake my head, holding up two fingers, he continues, "And I'm guessing they found your stuff?"

Massaging my temples, I shrug. "Some of it—a pair of shoes, a handbag, and my camera and its bag. Maybe they'll find some of the other things in pawnshops, but I seriously doubt it."

Wyatt yawns into his palm and then scratches his head. "At least they found the shitheads who did it," he says, and I nod my head in agreement. He stretches his arms over his head but then winces and glances down at the bandage over the right side of his muscular chest. "God, this hurts."

"Stop being such a baby, McCrae," I say, sticking my ring finger up at him. "I don't even feel a thing." Of course, that's a lie because as I move my finger around, pain shoots through my hand.

Snorting, Wyatt gives my thigh a squeeze, but I stop his fingers before he can go any further. "Really, Ky?" At first I think he's referring to me not letting him touch me, but then he grins and dips his head toward my new tattoo. "That little thing took all of thirty minutes."

It might have, but I can still tell from the look in his eyes how thrilled he is that I finally got Brad's last name wiped away from my body for good.

As I slide out of bed, Wyatt gives me one of those lingering looks that just makes me want to crawl back in and bury myself under the covers with him for the rest of the day. Taking a deep breath, I move my head slowly from side to side. "Don't you dare look at me like that," I warn. "Phoenix, remember?" I bend over to grab a change of clothes from my bag, feeling his eyes skim up my bare legs.

"Oh, I didn't forget about Phoenix. I'm just trying to figure out if you're wearing panties right now."

Tucking my clothes under my arm, I lift the hem of my oversized T-shirt to show him that I am in fact wearing underwear.

He flicks his tongue over his lip piercing as if I'm not. "We don't have to be in Phoenix until—"

Since I'm already making my way into the bathroom, I wave him off. "Get the hell up already."

He doesn't actually get out of bed until I come out of the shower, and I'm not surprised when he corners me in the bathroom. Instead of trying to convince me to keep my clothes off, he comes up behind me to help snap the closures of my delicate pink bra.

"I fucking hate Victoria's Secret," he murmurs when he fastens the last hook. He walks around my body, his palm skimming around my waist as he does so. When he kneels down in front of me, my breath catches, but then he reaches past me to grab my underwear from near the sink.

"But they have such pretty things," I tease.

"Yeah, but for me, it's torture." He strokes the outside of my foot, and I step into the pink panties he's holding out for me. He glides them up my smooth legs carefully, stopping just once to touch his lips against the inside of my thigh. I gasp, and then he gently tugs the flimsy fabric into place. "The worst type of torture imaginable."

"Sorry I can't just go commando all the time, babe."

Examining me for a long time, he finally lets out a low noise. "Hurry up and finish getting dressed before I rip those off of you and fuck you right here."

Cocking my eyebrow, I back away from him slowly, feeling the heat from his gaze as I grab my clothes from the hook behind the door. I shrug into them quickly, and he groans as I wiggle my hips a little to slide up my jeans.

"You're fucking killing me, beautiful," he says, pulling me to him by my belt loops.

"You should get dressed." Running my fingers along the elastic of his boxers, I slide my tongue over my lips. "By the way, you need to be more careful with all the ripping of the clothes. I'm starting to keep a mental note, and I'm billing your ass when we get to L.A." When I let the elastic snap against his waist, he sucks in a breath through his teeth.

"Bill me all you want as long as we get to fuck in the dressing room."

If he's trying to make me blush, he succeeds. He grins as he turns on the faucet, and I leave the bathroom quickly before he has a chance to try and talk me into taking a shower with him. With all this talk about ripping underwear and banging in dressing rooms, chances are I'd take him up on it.

***

As soon as he's finished showering, he sets about getting dressed. I watch him as he puts on a pair of relaxed dark jeans and a black T-shirt that not only accentuates his toned biceps but will also hide any bleeding ink on his chest. As soon as he's finished, he crosses the room to where I'm sitting on the edge of the bed. Leaning over me, he cups my face between his hands and kisses me. "You look beautiful, Ky."

"Didn't you know, McCrae?" I start, unable to keep the breathlessness out of my voice. "Your pretty words don't always make me drop my panties."

"Fuck . . . apparently not." He takes my hands in his and guides me toward the door to our room, tucking his hand into my back pocket as we walk down the hallway together. When I glance up at him, he grins at me, giving my ass a firm squeeze . "I'll try again after breakfast."

"You're a determined thing, aren't you?" I ask as we leave the hotel and walk in the direction of the restaurant where Heidi and I ate breakfast yesterday.

"Always." Just before we step through the restaurant door to join Heidi and Cal, he stops me, pulling my body flush to his. "But Kylie?"

"Wyatt?" We step to the right in sync to avoid a group of people making their way into the building. Our gazes stay locked for a long pause of time, until I lift an eyebrow. "You plan on speaking or continuing to creep me out with all the silence?"

He lowers his mouth to my ear. "Even if we don't fuck this morning, you're still beautiful." When he draws away from me, taking in my slightly stunned expression, a slow grin drags across his face. I make a noise in the back of my throat in an effort to clear away some of the tightness as I slide past him.

"So are you," I finally reply, pulling the restaurant door open.

Once we're seated, I order the same thing as before, the western omelet, and I promise myself that I'll actually enjoy my breakfast no matter who calls me. In fact, if my phone does ring, I'll send whoever it is directly to my voice mail.

Cal and Heidi are in deep conversation about something, but when I lift my coffee mug to my lips, he pauses. "What the hell is that on your finger?" From the way he's narrowing his brown eyes at the bandage, I'd think he didn't have a dozen tattoos of his own.

I take a sip of my coffee before answering him. The steaming liquid burns the tip of my tongue, and shooting Heidi an apologetic look, I grab her orange juice and take a giant sip in hopes that it will cool my mouth. Once I'm able to speak without slurring my words, I say, "New tattoo."

Despite being on the opposite side of the table, Heidi bends as close to me as she can to examine the clear wrapping around my finger. Her eyes widen, and she blurts out, "Jesus, Ky, did you two get married last night?"

Beside her, Cal chokes on his unsweetened tea and then garbles something incoherent.

Before either of them have a meltdown in the middle of the restaurant, I jump to correct Heidi's assumption. "I can promise you that we're definitely not married." I glance over at Wyatt. Although his shoulders are shaking from laughter, something flashes in his midnight blue eyes—curiosity.

My mind has wandered there before, thinking about what marriage would be like with Wyatt, but I won't let it go there again. Not when all the events of the last couple days have brought me closer to wanting to give things between the two of us one more try. Not when he's yet to tell me that he loves me.

No, marriage probably won't be something I stop and think about for a long time.

"I'm glad you didn't get married," Heidi announces, taking her orange juice away from me. "I would have punched you in the boob if I didn't get an invite."

\*\*\*

Once we're done with breakfast, we head back to the hotel to pack for Phoenix. We're on the road well before noon, and as Wyatt and I sit in the backseat together, his hand finds mine, clasping my fingers tightly.

"Last stop," he whispers, and I can only nod my head.

***

Heidi has to leave almost the moment we reach Phoenix six hours later. One of her brothers is already waiting for us at the hotel when Cal parks the SUV. She leaps out of the front seat of the Suburban and sprints across the parking lot, laughing as her brother gathers her up in a giant hug.

"He's fucking big," Cal says from beside me, eyeing Heidi and the tall beefy guy standing next to her. I tip my head in agreement. "I could probably take him."

Cocking an eyebrow, I glance at him from out of the corner of my eye. "Thought there was nothing going on between you two."

"Oh, there's not." He starts unloading our luggage, giving me a wink as he sets her suitcase on the asphalt. "But you never know what'll happen once we get back home."

*Right.* As I walk over to Heidi, I glance back at Cal once, and when I catch him staring at her, he drops his eyes.

Heidi reintroduces me to her brother, and as he climbs inside his ironically small sports car, she gives me a pained look. "So, apparently, my mom really went all out because I'm in town, and the entire family is coming over."

"Do you want me to go with you?"

She shakes her head, and I stifle a laugh at how dramatic the sad expression on her face is. "My nieces and nephews are possessed. After the last time you came home with me, I swore to you I'd never put you through that again."

I can't resist grinning. "Want me to wait around for you before I head over to the bar tonight?"

She bobs her head a little too enthusiastically. "I'm hoping it'll be sooner rather than later, but you know how my folks are." When her brother honks his horn, she rolls her eyes. "Ugh, see you later."

Before she gets into the car, she waves her arm dramatically to Wyatt and Cal to signal that she's leaving, and then I watch as her brother's sports car speeds away. Heidi can complain all she wants about her family, but I know better than anyone how much she adores them. Seeing them will be good for her.

Since Wyatt and Cal have a few things to take care of with the Hazard Anthem guys, I stay in our room after we check-in. The moment that Wyatt leaves, after promising me that he'll be back as soon as possible, I adjust the thermostat back to a normal temperature.

When I lie down to watch a marathon of *The Walking Dead,* I don't plan to fall asleep, but it's pretty much inevitable. The sound of Wyatt returning to the room gets me up, and I flick my eyes to the clock by the bed to see that it's 8:37 p.m.

Yawning, I sit up and swing my legs off the side of the bed. "Didn't realize it was so late." I smooth a bunch of stray pieces of my hair behind my ear. "Do I have time to get ready?"

He nods. "I've been calling you," he says, sitting down in the armchair across the room. "We go on in a little over an hour."

I grab my phone from the nightstand and release a groan when I realize it's dead. Since it's useless, I throw it down on the bed. "The battery in that thing sucks." If Wyatt's been trying to get in touch with me, chances are Heidi has, too. I rub my hand over my face in frustration. "Hey, you don't happen to have Heidi's number saved in your phone, do you?"

He shakes his head but pulls out his cell. He runs his finger up and down the screen, probably scrolling through his contacts. "Nope, but Cal does. He's having drinks with Nate and Ben, but he'll answer." He presses a button and then tosses the phone to me. I reach up and catch it easily with my right hand. "Going to wash my face before we get going. Be right back," he says, disappearing into the bathroom.

Just as Wyatt promised, Cal answers on the fourth ring. After he teases me about not knowing my best friend's number, he promises to text it to me as soon as we hang up. A moment after I hit the End button, the message comes through. "Impressive, Cal," I say, opening the text.

It takes me approximately five seconds to figure out that the string of messages I'm staring down at isn't from Cal, and even though I jab the Home button quickly, the last three texts between Terra and Wyatt have dug their way into my head.

6:29 p.m.: *You don't even want to know the room # in case you change your mind?*

7:01 p.m.: *I won't, so let's not waste our time. I told you the other night that it was one time. Fucking drop it.*

8:42 p.m.: ***You know what? Go fuck yourself, Wyatt.***

I hear the bathroom door ease open, and he's talking about Your Toxic Sequel's summer tour as he rounds the corner. My face must say it all because the moment he looks at me, his words fade away, and the color drains from his naturally tan face. Struggling to keep my breath steady, I stare into his eyes, and I repeat the question I asked him a couple nights ago, the question that I'm absolutely certain he answered with a flat-out lie.

"Did you screw Terra?"

# CHAPTER SIXTEEN

He lowers his dark blue eyes to the phone that's lying on the bed just as another text message comes through. I know that this time, it's probably Cal getting back to me with Heidi's number, but right now, that's the furthest thing from my mind. Right now, I desperately need to know the truth from the man standing in front of me.

"Did you lie to me?" I ask, standing. I take a tentative step toward him and then another, feeling my heart race faster and faster with each movement. Once my bare toes hit the toe of Wyatt's boot, I straighten my back. "Did you fuck Terra?"

Drawing his eyebrows together, he pinches his bottom lip between his thumb and forefinger. I never let my gaze fall even though I want to. At last, he swallows hard, giving me a brisk nod. "Yeah, I did."

I feel like something has collided into my chest, and I rub my hand back and forth over the center, hoping it will lessen the pain.

It doesn't. "And you've done it again since we came here? Since you and I have been together like this?"

Sucking in his upper lip, he shakes his head vigorously. "Absolutely not."

"Then, why not just tell me when I asked? Why make it a big secret?" He's had one-night stands before—and even though we weren't a couple, all those times ripped out my heart—but this is the first time he's lied to me. "Why didn't you just tell me the truth when I asked?" I demand, my voice cracking.

"Because you said her name like—"

My nostrils flare, and I hold up my hand. "Like what? Like I wanted to choke her? Who gives a damn how I said her name? All I wanted was for you to tell me the truth, to be straight with me. I can handle everything else, Wyatt." My shoulders begin to shake, and I drop my eyes to my bare feet. "When?" I ask.

"What?" he asks, his deep voice breaking.

"When did you do it?"

"Kylie, please." He holds out his hands, wanting to touch me, but I shove them away. I ignore the dull pain in my ring finger as I wait for him to answer me. When I release a sob, he exhales. "Why would you want to put yourself through that? Why does it even matter now?"

Of course, he doesn't understand. Maybe he never will. I take a few steps backward. "Because. You. Lied."

He drags his hand over his face, releasing a strangled noise from the back of his throat. "The end of last year."

I press myself against the wall for support. "Let me guess, it was a couple of weeks after Thanksgiving, huh?" His expression is blank, and I immediately realize that I've called it accurately. Clenching my teeth, I shake my head to each side. "You are so goddamn unbelievable, Wyatt."

His face flushes as he takes a step toward me. "You push me away at every turn. You told me you wanted to see other people. What the—"

"You're right," I say, nodding my head. "You're absolutely right. But if you still want to know why I stopped calling you after Thanksgiving...there, you've got your answer. I thought..." I pause and take a deep breath. "I guess you were too busy fucking Terra when I needed you."

This time, when he reaches out to touch me, he succeeds. He draws me to his chest, not seeming to care about the pain it might cause to the area where he got the bluebird tattoo last night. "What were you going to say, Ky? You thought what?" he demands.

Since we're laying it all out on the table tonight, I glare up at him. "I thought I was pregnant. I thought that I was going to have a kid with someone who can't even say he loves me, and I panicked."

His grip tightens on the small of my back. "You're not, are you?" The tone of his voice is low and dangerous, and I know he's thinking about all the partying we've done over the past few days. "Are you?" he says more urgently.

I shake my head. "Do you really think I'm that stupid and selfish?" I ask. I close my eyes, squeezing them so tight that the tears have no other choice but to stay put. He releases a long exhale, but when I speak a moment later, he loses his breath once more. "Wyatt...I really can't do this anymore."

He clenches his jaw. "Yes, you can. I fucked up. I know that I did, but that doesn't mean we can't fix ourselves." When he touches his forehead against mine, I pull away from him, pressing my back to the wall again.

"I've done exactly what I told you I'd do. I came here with you. I let you remind me of our past, the good and the bad. But, Wyatt, I just *can't* anymore." Each word takes an excruciating amount of effort, and I know that if we don't end this soon, I'm going to be sick to my stomach.

"We can fix this, Ky," he says.

I shake my head again, wiping tears from my cheeks. "We've been doing this for so long," I whisper. "After Brenna and my ex and so much bullshit, it's amazing we didn't already give up on each other years ago. Don't you see it? If we haven't fixed ourselves by now, how the hell do you think we ever can?"

"I refuse to believe that." He's breathing heavily, his chest rising and falling against mine. "I love you, Kylie."

The sob that I've been so successfully holding back finally makes its way past my throat, and I gasp. I lower my head, shaking it slowly, as my shoulders tremble. He's dealt me the most painful blow of all, and surely, he must know that because he backs away from me slowly. When I manage to lift my gaze, the agony in his blue eyes matches the sting spreading across my chest, consuming me.

"Fuck, I mean, you had to have known that already," he says hoarsely.

I press my hand to my chest for a moment, pushing hard as if it will stop my heart from pounding so rapidly, as if doing so will keep me from crumbling apart. Once I've managed to control my tears, I say, "I have waited so goddamn long to hear you say that, and now that I have…it just hurts." It hurts because of all times to tell me that he loves me, he picks the one moment when losing me is a certainty.

Closing his eyes, he wrings his strong hands together. "That's not my intention."

"If you say so, Wyatt," I say in a detached voice. Rubbing the heel of my palm over my eyes to wipe away the remaining dampness from my face, I take a deep breath. "Your show starts soon."

"It can wait."

I think back to the day I asked him if he planned on leaving Your Toxic Sequel, and my vision blurs. "Did you lie about that, too? About quitting YTS?" His lowered blue eyes and silence is all the answer I need. "God, Wyatt…"

"I'm not," he argues. He eases down onto the edge of the bed, darting his blue eyes over to where I'm still standing, clutching the wall. "Things were going shitty, okay? Lucas is a dick, and Sinjin's always fucked-up. Cal and I were both thinking about bailing last year, but we changed our minds, okay? When Hazard Anthem called us about doing these shows, I figured we owed them one for leaving them high and dry."

I fold my arms over my chest, giving him a tight smile. "You don't need to explain yourself to me. I get it. It's business." I'm not going to argue with him anymore. There's no point because I already know that I'll have to leave.

"Will you be here when I get back tonight?"

His eyes are pleading, and I have difficulty speaking past the pain in the back of my throat.

"You already know that I won't."

"God, Kylie. Don't do this," he begs. "I'm sorry."

"Have a good show, Wyatt," I say softly, turning away from him.

I feel like weights are tied to my shoulders as I walk into the bathroom. I close the door behind me, lean my head against it, and start counting as I wait for him to leave. I hear the door to our room slam shut when I reach 150, and I press my fist to my mouth as sobs shake my entire body.

***

I'm packing and crying when Heidi shows up at my door an hour later. Her grin quickly fades as soon as I open the door. She doesn't ask questions. She doesn't try to give me advice. She simply yanks me to her, wrapping her thin arms around me.

"Is that ride back home still on the table?" I whisper.

She nods against my shoulder. "For you, babe, anything."

# CHAPTER SEVENTEEN

I'm back in L.A. before the sun even rises the next morning, and I spend the rest of my weekend alone, leaving my apartment only once to go to the market around the corner. It's not as if I'm in a catatonic state because I'm a seasoned pro at dealing with this type of bullshit, but the last thing I want is to bring someone else's mood down with my moping around.

Later that night, I make plans with Heidi to take me to the DMV office first thing tomorrow morning.

\*\*\*

When my doorbell rings at seven thirty in the morning on the dot, I'm already dressed. After brushing the tangles out of my black-and-blue hair, I fling open the door, and I'm shocked when I see my brother standing on the other side, holding a box from my favorite bakery.

"I didn't realize you knew where I lived," I say sarcastically, ignoring the way my stomach growls as I step backward to let him inside.

Ducking his head because he's so damn tall, he comes through the doorway and makes a face at me. "Don't look so fucking happy to see me next time." He follows me into my den. "Brought you your favorite," he says as he slams down into the chair at my computer desk, setting the box beside my laptop.

"Heidi's taking me to the DMV to get a new license in a little bit, so can you make this quick?"

He grabs my phone from the desk and then rolls the chair forward until he stops right in front of me. "Call her and cancel."

I take the phone, but instead of making the call, I cross my arms over my chest. "Lucas, I take my job very, *very* seriously, but it's impossible for me to drive your ass around if I don't have a license."

"Cute," he says, dragging his lips up into a strained smile. "But I'm here to take you to the DMV myself."

I'm momentarily stunned. Being up so early is typical for my brother—he works out for a couple hours every morning—but for some reason, he's taken it upon himself to visit me. And now, he's offering to help me complete a tedious task that I don't even want to do myself. Cocking my head to the side, I pull my eyebrows together. "Dude, you're scaring the shit out of me. Is everything alright?"

His smile suddenly becomes more forced, and he leans forward, supporting his arms on his thighs. "Abso-fucking-lutely not, Kylie. I've made a mess of things."

Taking the bakery box off the desk, I go to the other side of the small room and sit down on my couch. Half a dozen glazed doughnuts are in the box, and I sigh, inhaling their sweet scent. I eat two before I ask him about Sienna. "Have you talked to her?"

He squeezes his hazel eyes closed and shakes his head, dragging one of his hands through his shaggy dark hair. "You know better than I do that she's already changed her number."

I nod my head in acknowledgment and swallow hard, nearly choking on a piece of my doughnut. "Did you try to call her before she changed her number?"

"No. What the fuck would I say?"

"Sorry is a start."

He snorts. "Sorry doesn't even begin to cover what I did to her, Kylie." Sitting upright, he checks his watch before giving me a pointed look. "DMV opens in twenty minutes. Let's not bullshit, so we don't have to stick around there all day."

"I didn't ask you to take me," I say in a heated voice as I pull up Heidi's number on my iPhone.

She answers drowsily on the third ring. "Ah, shit." She yawns, and I hear her roll over in her bed. "I worked late and forgot to set my alarm."

"It's okay! Lucas is here to take me to get my new license, but I'll stop by your place tonight or something."

My best friend is quiet for several seconds, and I imagine she's just as stunned as I am about my brother showing up at my apartment. "Um, okay. Let me know how that one goes."

I glimpse over at Lucas as he's rubbing the pads of his thumbs against his temples in frustration. "It should be interesting." After I promise Heidi that I'll call her the moment I'm done taking care of my personal business today, I end the call.

Lucas stands up, taking his car key out of his pocket. "You done?" His voice is sardonic.

I hold back a sharp reply as I nod and close the doughnut box. "I'm ready." As he heads to the front door, I grab my folder of paperwork from my desk and start to join him, but then I stop. I glance down at my ring finger, which has started to scab. There's no point in me going to the DMV just to get another license that says *Kylie Martin*. "Hey, Lucas?" I call out.

"Yeah?"

"How long does it take to do a name change on your social security card? Is it right away?"

Even from the other room, I can hear him make a frustrated noise. "Google is your friend. Look it up yourself." Even though he can't see me, I glare daggers in his general direction, literally biting my tongue, as I sit behind the desk and open my laptop.

After a few minutes of research, I discover that getting a new social security card will take several days. Since I obviously can't wait for a new license, I make myself a note, so I'll remember to take care of the name change another day. *The sooner, the better.*

\*\*\*

\

Instead of using the parking garage, Lucas has left his car on the curb, and I lift an eyebrow as we walk down the steps toward the brand new Audi. This is the first time I've seen it. I didn't even realize he had bought a new car.

"Sam get you a gift with your money?" I ask.

He narrows his hazel eyes into dangerous slits. "Kylie, I swear to God—"

I climb into my seat, cutting off his threat by slamming my door. As I wait for him to get inside the car, I turn toward the driver's seat. He's still glaring at me when he closes his door and presses his fingertip on the push start.

"Maybe this was a bad idea," he growls, but I shake my head. The more I think about it, Lucas randomly picking me up is a very good thing.

"No, this talk has been a long time coming. I can't believe I waited so long before saying something, but I am now."

In typical Lucas fashion, he automatically gets defensive. "You want to talk about Wyatt then? Since we're sharing our feelings."

I press my lips into a thin line. Of course, I don't want to talk about Wyatt. It hurts like hell to even think about that man, but I know it's something that I'll eventually have to acknowledge. Just because he lied to me doesn't change the fact that I still love him. Just because I walked away from him doesn't change the fact that I'll have to see him again when I'm working.

"Ask away," I tell my brother, squaring my shoulders.

He pulls the Audi into traffic. "Alright. What happened?"

"Why would you assume something did?"

He gives me a hard stare. "Because he called me and wanted to know if you were okay. Apparently, I'm the go-to guy on all things Kylie Wolfe."

My chest tightens as I run my fingers through my hair nervously. "And?"

"I lied. I told him I saw you yesterday morning, and you were the happiest I've ever seen you."

For what seems like an eternity, we sit in traffic, completely silent. Once I digest what Lucas has just told me, I clear my throat. "I'm not sure if I should say thank you or be irritated."

"Irritated because I finally stepped in and tried to do something to stop you two from hurting each other?"

"Yeah, irritated that after eight years, you're just now showing an interest in your kid sister's personal life."

"You don't think I give a shit about what's happening with you? You're my sister. Don't ever think for one second that I don't love you, you got me?" When I nod, he adds, "I just want you to be happy."

My throat constricts, and I clench my fists. "Thanks, Lucas." My voice is hoarse, and he turns his head slightly, giving me a sad smile, as he touches my shoulder. "I love you, too," I say.

Even though I want nothing more right now than to stay with him in the car and talk to him about Samantha, he pulls the Audi into the DMV lot, parking the car in the farthest spot from the entrance.

"Lucas," I say before I get out. He cocks one of his thick eyebrows. "When I'm done in here, we're going to talk about you."

He doesn't move or say anything, but he doesn't have to. I know that I'll be able to get something out of him even if it's not the absolute truth.

*** 

Since I have all the documents I need to get a new license, the whole process from start to finish takes less than an hour, which is like a miracle for the DMV. My brother looks surprised when I slide into the Audi.

He tucks his phone back into his pocket. "Let me guess, you're missing shit?" he demands. I shake my head and flip open my wallet to show him my new card. He moves his head from side to side incredulously as he starts the car. "And I can bet money when I have to come in and get my renewal, it'll take me all day long."

During the short drive back to my apartment, I think of several different ways to approach the subject of Sam with Lucas. It's so ridiculously easy to ruin my brother's mood that I want to approach it carefully.

Then, I look at him. I study the way his shoulders sag and how his hazel eyes just seem tired. And I realize that there's no way in hell I can ruin his day any worse than he already has.

"We're a fucked-up pair," I say quietly after he parks near the curb.

He releases a strangled laugh. "Yeah, we are." He leans his head back against his headrest, inhaling and exhaling deeply. "I wanted to make things work with her so fucking bad," he says, referring to Sienna.

I nod. "You still can, but you're going to have to let go of whatever it is Sam's got on you. You know that, don't you?"

"It's not that fucking simple."

"Then, let me help you. Tell me what she has on you, so we can figure it out together," I plead. He shakes his head, refusing me. "I promise I'm not going to stop loving you." When he doesn't reply as he stares straight ahead through the windshield, my chest clenches. "Lucas, it's not something that will make me stop loving you," I say again, but this time, it sounds more like a question than a statement.

He's quiet for much longer than necessary, and when he answers me, my heart aches so much more for him. "No, it's not, but only because it's not in you to stop loving someone."

# CHAPTER EIGHTEEN

For the next week, Wyatt calls my cell phone twice a day, once in the afternoon and then again at night. He doesn't leave messages, and he doesn't send texts. I'm sure he knows that I'm purposely missing his calls every time I send him straight to voice mail. It's so hard to do that to him because each time I hit the top button on my iPhone to ignore the call, it feels like a hole is being burned into my chest.

Nine days after my return from Phoenix, my brother calls me a little after noon. "You busy?" Lucas asks the moment I pick up. He sounds out of breath, like he's been lifting weights. Before I can answer him, he continues, "I got an email this morning about some sponsorship thing you signed me up for. Want to check into it for me?"

Lucas has been trying to keep me as busy as possible since I came home to L.A., and while I appreciate his concern, his hovering is starting to become slightly annoying. I save the letter that I've been writing to Sinjin. "I'm on it right now," I say as I pull up his Gmail account.

"Call me after you figure it out, okay?"

After I promise that I will, he ends the call, and I scroll through his inbox in search of the email. I find it near the top of his message list, where he told me it would be, so I open it up and begin to read.

According to the email, the organization, which provides sports equipment to disadvantaged kids, has left a message for his assistant. Wrinkling my forehead, I bite the inside of my lip because I haven't received any calls from them. I head to the kitchen and grab a bottle of water, and then I sit back down to do a little more research.

It's not until I find a thread of old correspondence with the group from months ago that I realize I gave them the direct number to my apartment instead of my cell phone number. The only phone I keep in my place is located in my bedroom, and since I went the quirky novelty route when I purchased it, it's corded. I sit on my bed with my laptop in front of me to take notes as I check the message.

Sure enough, there's a voice mail from the organization that's dated back to a week ago. I listen to it twice, typing down all the pertinent information I'll need for Lucas to make a donation. I erase the message, and I'm about to hang up, but then the next voice mail automatically starts playing.

The voice on the line sends chills through my body. It's Wyatt. For ten minutes, I find myself listening to messages he left for me while we were in New Orleans before he realized he was calling the wrong number. It isn't until I reach the sixth voice mail that I feel as if my lungs have completely failed me.

"Do you ever pick up your goddamn phone, beautiful?" Wyatt asks in a low, sexy voice, and my breath catches painfully. "I need you to be there next week, Ky. I need to know that I'll see you when I come to Nashville to start recording because this separation bullshit has been going on for too long. Look, I know that you're pissed because of my last message, but I can't help the past. I can't change how fucked-up we've been to each other. I just want to make things right now." There's a muffled noise, and I hear Cal's voice. Wyatt mutters something under his breath, and then he clears his throat. "Call me when you're ready. And Kylie? I love you, okay?"

It feels like butterflies are racing though my stomach as I wrap my fingers around the cord tightly, listening carefully as the automated voice speaks the time and date. He left the message the last week of January, a couple of weeks before he found me in New Orleans. My mouth goes dry, and I swallow several times.

Saving the voice mail, I start the next, which turns out to be a telemarketer. I go through two more spam calls before I find Wyatt's other message.

"I fucked up. I've fucked up, and it's something I don't ever want to do again. I don't want other women. I want *you*. It's been that way for as long as I can remember, and it's going to stay that way. We need to make a decision. We're either together or apart, but no more of this bullshit that we've been doing to each other for the past few years. It's destructive, and it's time we stop pretending like we can just be friends with benefits or whatever the hell you're calling it now.

"I love you, Kylie. You know I have a hard time saying that, but I do. Stop ignoring my calls, stop being so afraid of getting hurt, and let's figure this out."

The message ends there, and I feel numb as I listen to the date and time, learning that he left this particular voice mail back in December. I slide my laptop to the other side of my bed and carefully place the phone back on the receiver, as if it will break at the slightest harsh movement. I stare at the nightstand, at the phone. And I sit in silence like I'm waiting, like I'm expecting the phone to ring at any moment.

When nothing happens and the quietness continues, I close my eyes tightly. I can almost hear Wyatt's voice in my head, telling me over and over again that he loves me.

"I love you, too," I finally whisper.

***

Wyatt's messages stay in the front of my mind for the next few days, and it's nearly impossible for me to get much done besides writing Sinjin two more letters and going to the gym with Heidi once.

When my cell phone rings on Friday afternoon and my mom's voice comes on the line, a wave of relief washes through my body. She's got this way of making me feel better by just saying a couple of words, and I stretch out on my sofa as I talk to her.

"You sound tired," she points out in a worried voice.

Even though she can't see me, I shake my head. "Just a little stressed."

After she reminds me that I need to take better care of myself, she changes the subject to my upcoming trip to Atlanta to see her and my dad. "Are you still planning to visit in a few weeks?"

"I'll be there, driving you insane," I promise. When she laughs, I imagine her grinning face and how she's probably waving her hand, shaking my comment off.

"You could never do that, baby. Me and your dad just really…" She pauses for several seconds, and a sob hitches in my throat. The moment she opens her mouth to speak again, the concern has returned along with the firm voice she used on us when we were kids. "Alright, spill it now."

And I do. Even though my mother is a youth pastor, I leave nothing out, telling her about everything from the cutting to all the years of constant drama with Wyatt and even about the messages I recently discovered. When I'm done, she's quiet for a long time.

"Do you love him?" she asks. "Are you still in love with Wyatt McCrae?"

Lucas's words from the day at the DMV come to mind, and I swallow hard because my brother was right. It is impossible for me to stop loving someone. "Of course I do. I'll never stop."

My mother makes a squeaking noise, like she's worrying her lip between her teeth. I hear her say something to my dad, and then I hear the sound of a door closing. "Then, you need to tell him that. If you both love each other, you need to be committed. And if he's not willing to do that...well, the least you can do is get everything off your chest."

"I don't even know if it could work," I say.

I can practically hear her shaking her head when she responds to me. "You don't know anything until you try. No relationship is perfect, and there won't ever be one that is. You just have to figure out how to fix yours."

"I'll contact him."

"You don't sound so sure," she says, so when I respond, my voice is firm and convincing.

"I'm going to go see him, Mom. Even if we can't be together, you're right. Not trying will hurt so much worse than talking to him and agreeing that it's best we stay apart."

She releases a sigh of relief. "Good, I'm so proud of you. I've got to hang up now—your dad and I have made plans this evening, but I love you. I've loved you and Lucas since the day you were born, been proud of you both since I first laid eyes on you, and nothing will ever change that." Before we end the call, she clears her throat softly. "And Kylie? There's so much we need to talk about in person when you come home."

I've given her a lot to think about and said things I never planned on revealing to her, so I know by the time I go to Atlanta, we'll have hours of conversation ahead of us. There might be tears and maybe even some angry words, but I nod my head, welcoming it. "I know, Mom. I love you, too."

***

For the next twenty-four hours, I think on my mom's words quite a bit, and by the next evening, I know that I'm ready to face Wyatt. I don't want to lose my nerve, so I don't call him to let him know I'm on my way as I make the drive to his West Hollywood bungalow.

His car, a fully restored classic Chevelle, is parked in his driveway, and I pull my blue Yaris right behind it. Taking a deep breath, I walk up to his front door. I ring the bell and then clench my fists by my side as I wait for him to answer.

When he pulls open the door a moment later, he's speaking to someone over his shoulder, but his words are cut off the second he lays his intense blue eyes on me.

Slowly, I take in the sight of him. He's barefoot, wearing nothing but a pair of gym shorts. My gaze traces over the bluebird tattoo on his chest. It's healing fast, and I feel a sharp pang in my rib cage. "Hey, I hope you don't mind me—"

"God, no. Never. Come in." He's hesitant to touch me at first, but then he places his palms to the side of my face, pushing back soft wisps of my hair with his thumbs. I tilt my face up to his, not caring that it's obvious I'm breathing in the subtle scent of his cologne. "I can't believe you're here," he murmurs at last as he lowers his hands.

He moves aside, and I smile and step into his foyer. He stares at me for a long time until a noise from the hallway makes him turn his eyes away. "Be right there," he calls out over his shoulder.

"You're busy," I say, suddenly feeling stupid. "I can come back later. I can—"

But the other person in the house hears me and cuts me off by saying my name loudly. "Kylie?"

It's Brenna's voice, and I lift my head to take in the sight of her just as she comes rushing from the hallway. She runs into me, hard, knocking the air out of my lungs.

# CHAPTER NINETEEN

"Jesus, kid, you're getting tall," I say. I close my arms around the girl clinging to my waist and hold her close. "Next year, you'll be my height."

Pulling away from me, she makes a face, and I screw my own into a dramatic pout. We both hold the looks for a long time before she gives up and laughter bubbles from her chest. I'm too nervous to laugh, so I manage a little smile as I tuck a lock of her dark blonde hair behind her ear.

"You're just fun-sized," Brenna says. She glances over at Wyatt, who hasn't moved since she came sprinting into the foyer. "You said Kylie was gone on vacation, Dad."

He lifts his shoulders slightly, and his eyes search my face, waiting for me to have some type of reaction toward him. "Guess she came back early."

Brenna beams up at me. "Did you have fun?"

I fold my arms across my stomach, holding myself together. "It was…" I search for the right word, but it doesn't come to me. I lift my eyes, finally meeting Wyatt's deep stare head-on. "I'm glad to be home."

She bobs her head up and down, grabbing my hand to lead me into Wyatt's living room. Knocking a couple of PlayStation 3 controllers aside, she motions for me to sit beside her on the tan leather couch. Since I've never been able to say no to Brenna, I comply. "So, where all did you go?" she demands.

"New Orleans."

"Lots of good food?"

"Are you kidding? Some of the best." I catch Wyatt's blue eyes as he eases down onto the matching loveseat across from us. I wonder if Brenna knows he was in New Orleans with me for a short period of time, but when he gives me a slight shake of his head, I figure he hasn't told her. "Your dad will have to take you there some day."

She looks at him expectantly, and he gives her a halfhearted grin. Returning her attention to me, she proudly declares, "Mom's planning on taking me to Orlando this summer while Dad's on tour."

"You going to ride the teacups until you get sick?" I tease.

She wrinkles her nose. "I'm too old for that. I do get to go and see Hog—"

"Baby," Wyatt says softly, cutting off Brenna. She lifts her eyebrows impatiently, waiting for him to continue. Wearing that tender smile he's always reserved exclusively for her, he comes across the room to kneel down in front of us. "Kylie and I need to talk right now. Can you go in your room for a little bit?"

She presses her small lips together and starts to shake her head. Then, she reconsiders, and a slow grin that looks just like his builds on her face. "Pizza for dinner? And *then* you help me beat that level in my game?"

He groans, moving his head from side to side, as he contemplates her offer. "Deal," he says, surprising both Brenna and me. He's never been a fan of pizza or video games. "Give me twenty minutes, okay?"

Wearing a look of sheer satisfaction, she leaves the room, and I watch her disappear down the hallway until she closes the door to her bedroom. I rub the pad of my thumb over the first blackbird tattoo, which is located a few inches over my left breast. I got it after

Wyatt had confessed to getting a one-night stand pregnant. He'd met her a few months after we'd first made love in that hotel in Livingston, and even though we hadn't been a couple and we'd agreed that we weren't seeking a relationship, finding out that he had a baby on the way stung so much that I didn't speak to him for months.

I didn't actually meet Brenna until a couple of months after he had come looking for me once I had divorced Brad. Seeing her in person made me instantly regret that first tattoo. Brenna wasn't one of the letdowns over the last several years.

She's a piece of him that I've always loved fiercely.

"She's an amazing kid," I murmur, rubbing my hand across my chest.

As he slides down beside me on the couch, I drop my eyes to his hands. They're in his lap, clenched, and I can almost guess he's wondering why I'm here. "I'm not sure what to say, Ky." His midnight blue eyes skim over my face, as if he's trying to read my expression. "I fucked up, and I'm sorry."

Because I'm not ready to touch what happened in Phoenix quite yet, I change the subject quickly. "Courtney dropping her off for the night?" I ask, referring to Brenna's mother.

He makes a noise in the back of his throat. "Courtney's taking a vacation with her new boyfriend. She'll be back in a few weeks."

I frown because I know that the obvious irritation in his voice doesn't stem from jealousy or not wanting to take care of Brenna—he adores that kid. I'm almost one hundred percent sure he's frustrated with Courtney because of the way his own mother left him when he was a kid. His bitterness over those memories is one of the reasons why he's always been such a huge part of Brenna's life. "I'm glad I got to see her. I've missed her," I say, staring in the direction of the hallway. I can hear music blasting from Brenna's room, some bubblegum boy band. "I'm surprised you even let her listen to that while she's here," I tease, trying to lighten the mood, and he laughs.

"You're all she's talked about since she came here. She's missed you." He lifts his hands, dragging them through his blond hair. "Fuck, I miss you, Ky."

"It's only been eleven days," I point out, my voice shaking.

"That wasn't eleven days, not when I've spent them thinking you were gone, Kylie. That was fucking agony."

I stand, clenching my hands together, as I pace in front of the big screen TV. "I didn't plan to come here, McCrae. I was more than done with you because you lied to me, and then…" My chest tightens up, and I take a deep breath, staring at his bare feet, as he gets up and comes to me.

When he touches my shoulders, I shiver. "So, what changed?" He glides his hands up, so that he can tilt my chin, and I'm forced to meet him eye-to-eye.

"I checked my home voice mail, and message after message was from you. You said things that I've only imagined you saying."

"And so you came here?"

I laugh, but it sounds more like a hysterical gasp. "No. I rearranged my apartment. I wrote a bunch of letters to Sinjin. I played my guitar. Finally, my mother called—"

He stops me from continuing, pressing his rough thumbs to my lips, as the rest of his fingers massage the sides of my face.

"Thought you forgot how to play," he says in a low voice. "At least, that's what you said back in Albuquerque."

"No." I shake my head. "I'd never forget."

He releases a deep exhale, crushing me to his chest. "Everything that I said in those messages? I meant every goddamn word. For you and that kid in there..." He points in the direction of Brenna's bedroom. "I'd do anything. I'd give up the music and the lifestyle if you asked me to."

A bitter ache spreads across the center of my chest. "I would never ask you to do that. You know that, don't you? I would never make you choose between me and what you love."

"You are what I love, Ky." Dropping his hands to my shoulders, he continues. "I don't know what you want from this anymore, but I know what I need. That's you. And don't try to bullshit me into thinking that you don't need me, too. You wouldn't be here if you didn't."

"It's not that simple," I whisper.

He shakes his head. "I don't believe that for a second." His voice, eyes, and even his touch are slowly breaking my heart. "All I know is that you're all I think about. I can't *not* have you in my life because you and Brenna are the only two people who give a shit about me."

"Still doesn't make it simple, babe." Dragging my palm across the center of my chest, I close my eyes. "I was stupid for thinking that I could just walk away from us and pretend like the last eight years had never happened. It's impossible."

He bends his head, so our lips are practically touching. "Then, we start over and fix things."

"It won't be easy, and it sure as hell won't be quick," I point out.

He shrugs. "Nothing worthwhile ever is." As I take a second to digest what he just said, he inches his mouth a little closer. His piercing touches my bottom lip, sending a ripple of pleasure through me. "I fucking love you, Ky. That's about all I need to know. We can work through all the other shit as long as we have that."

Even though he's said it before, both in the messages he left for me and on the night we argued in Phoenix, hearing him tell me that he loves me now takes my breath away. Somehow, I manage to force my voice to sound confident when I respond. "I love you, too."

*So much that I'll put myself out there one last time to see if one four-letter emotion is enough.*

His muscular shoulders sag in relief as he grips me closer to him. He kisses me. It's a simple yet powerful touch that lasts no longer than ten seconds. "I'm not perfect, Ky. I'll never be because I'm fucked-up, but I don't want to hurt you again."

"I know you don't," I say. Ignoring the nervous fluttering in the pit of my stomach, I circle my arms around him tighter, losing myself in the way he holds me to him.

"Can I come out now?" Brenna shrieks from the back over the sound of boy band falsetto.

"Not listening to that you can't," he bellows, and she cuts the music abruptly.

"Happy, Dad?"

I can't help but laugh as I wipe the backs of my hands over my cheeks to get rid of the tears that have started to fall.

"We're good now," Wyatt yells back.

Her bedroom door flies open, and she races down the hallway, jumping onto the couch. She ignores Wyatt's pointed frown and eyes me suspiciously. "Is everything okay?"

I glance at Wyatt and then to her. "It's going to be."

"Are you staying for dinner?"

"If your dad is paying."

We both focus our gazes—her blue eyes and my brown—on Wyatt until he nods his head. "But we order in tonight," he says, and she suppresses a groan. "And no making Kylie play that fuc—"

"Dad!" she says sharply.

He groans. "*Your* video game."

\*\*\*

Much later in the evening, after Brenna falls asleep on the floor playing her video game, Wyatt goes to the back room. He returns a few minutes later, holding two guitars, and then he extends one out to me. At first, I start to decline since Brenna's only a few feet away, but he places the Fender in my lap. Taking my hands in his, he wraps my fingertips around the neck of the custom black guitar.

He sits across the room from me on the loveseat, gripping his guitar, and a tiny smile builds on my lips when he strums the opening of "Send the Pain Below." It's one of those songs that I'll never forget, that will always have a special meaning for me, but it seems so wrong when we're supposed to be trying again.

Grabbing my pick off the side table, I start playing a new song. He pauses, and it takes him a moment to figure out the chords I'm struggling to strum through. Even though he doesn't know it well because he's never been an Incubus fan, he catches on quickly as we pick through the song about love surviving the bad things.

When we reach the last line of the song, I can't help but sing along softly. "Without love, I won't survive."

His eyes never leave mine, and I think about our bad times and our good. I'm hopeful that, this time, things will work, so we can make new memories that won't hurt so damn much.

Still, I savor every part of our past.

# THE SAVOR YOU PLAYLIST

1. "Love Hurts" by Incubus

2. "Lonely Boy" by The Black Keys

3. "Future Starts Slow" by The Kills

4. "Say It Ain't So" by Weezer

5. "The Red" by Chevelle

6. "All Lips Go Blue" by HIM

7. "Falling" by The Civil Wars

8. "Crazy on You" by Heart

9. "Love the Way You Lie" by Skylar Grey

10. "I Miss the Misery" by Halestorm

11. "Send the Pain Below" by Chevelle

12. "I Get It" by Chevelle

13. "Sweet Nothing" by Calvin Harris, Featuring Florence Welch

14. "Try" by P!nk

15. "By the Way" by Theory of a Deadman

16. "Fade into You" by Mazzy Star

17. "The Promise" by In This Moment

18. "Careless Whisper" by Seether

19. "One More Night" by Maroon 5

20. "Love-Hate-Sex-Pain" by Godsmack

21. "You" by The Pretty Reckless

22. "Never Let This Go" by Paramore

# WARNING

The following page contains an exclusive bonus scene from the novel *Devoured* told from Lucas Wolfe's point of view. If you have not read the book, please be advised that the scene contains major spoilers.

# *DEVOURED* BONUS SCENE

## EPILOGUE

### *LUCAS WOLFE*

It's exactly 8:57 p.m., when I ease my Audi A8 off the highway and down Sienna's driveway. It's almost dark outside, but someone—I'm betting her grandmother—has installed two rows of solar lights, courtesy of Home Depot, down the length of the path, leading all the way up to the front steps. I start to drive forward, letting the slight glow from the garden lights draw me in to Sienna, but then I think better of it.

I need her to be surprised.

I shift the car into park and kill the ignition. When I get out, quietly closing the Audi's door so Si won't hear me, I realize that I'm closer to the road than to the cabin. It's ironic when I think about it because at one time, this entire damn property had belonged to me. I'd wagered it away to get Sienna close to me, and in the end, I lost both because of fear and stupidity.

"Fucking idiot," I mutter to myself as I begin to make my way to her front door. I've timed my arrival precisely, but I still feel like I'm horribly late, like I've already ruined shit all over again before I even had the chance to fix it.

On the way over here, I thought about getting flowers or a gift, but I axed that idea quickly. Sienna has never been that type of person. She'll either take my apology, or she'll tell me to piss off, but she doesn't want what my money can buy.

She's not like Samantha.

Silently, I go up the front steps and across the covered porch to lean in close to the door. I can hear the sound of my own music from inside—my first solo project, my first *real* attempt to fix something I had fucked up to pieces since the "Sam Days." Even though Sienna's hearing me out by giving the song a chance, I can't force myself to relax while I wait for it to end. Hell, my chest feels like I've swallowed a shot glass full of acid. I am not a stranger to pain—it's all I feel whenever I see my ex, whenever I let her pull my strings—but I never expected the last five months to be this goddamn bad. This is different.

But, of course, I never expected to fall so damn hard for Sienna.

Inside the cabin, the music finally fades to silence. It's so quiet that I'm able to hear her take in a deep breath. I know she's waiting for more, just like I want her to, and I know that I've got to be the one to give her that—face-to-face.

Even though I've played shows in front of thousands of people, I'm nervous as hell when I knock on the door. She takes a long time to answer, and I almost feel like she's not going to. Sienna's smart, so there's a good chance she already knows that I'm the one out here, waiting for her. She knows that in my eyes, her not opening the door will be a bigger *fuck you* than her saying the words directly to my face.

But at last, the door creeps open a couple inches and then a few more until I can see her face. Adrenaline compels me to finish the song I wrote for her, the song I purposely left unfinished just so this one last piece could belong to just the two of us. Sinjin, my drummer, called it a pussy move, but he could go fuck himself.

"Say that what happened isn't it for us," I breathe, running my hand along the curve of her face.

Sienna looks just as goddamn beautiful as she did the last time I saw her when I left our hotel room in Atlanta. Except now, instead of a slinky dress I want to rip apart just to get to the center of her, she's wearing a white tank top and tiny denim shorts that make her legs seem impossibly longer. Now, her red hair is pulled into a tight ponytail and not loose, the way I like it. But the expression on her face is the same as it was when I left her last—wide-eyed and afraid. She's sliding her teeth back and forth, and I feel like a bastard for doing this to her.

"What are you doing here, Lucas?" she whispers, tucking a stray strand of hair behind her ear as she shrugs away from my touch.

*I'm here to tell you that I'm so sorry. I want to say I love you.*

Instead, I murmur in a rough voice, "You've got two days left."

Her mouth drops open, but she quickly closes it, swallows hard, and glares at me. "You *dismissed* me." She says it in a voice that makes me feel like she thinks I've forgotten.

*If only she knew.* The moment I sent her away from me is something that will never leave my mind, no matter how many years pass or how many people come and go in my life. That moment had gone on my short list of regrets before I even reached the elevator outside of our hotel room.

When she takes a step backward into the house, I know that I'm losing this, losing her, and this is something I can't afford to lose because I need her.

"You signed a contract," I remind her. It's a low move, one that causes her to shake her head in disbelief. Softening my tone, I add, "And I'm a fucking idiot."

Admitting I'm wrong helps because not only does her wide blue gaze dart up to mine as a choked noise comes from the back of her throat, she also makes a hesitant move in my direction, and then she makes another.

*One step backward and two steps forward.*

I can deal with that happening if it means that she'll eventually be close to me.

"I'm not going to give this up," I tell her, curling my fingers around her wrist and yanking her to me. She smells so fucking good, like that apple body wash she's used since before we first met. "I'm not going to give you up," I say.

*Because I'll always want her.*

As her lips part, a broad range of emotions pass over her face—lust and anger, fear and *pain*. My chest constricts again because I'm fully aware that I'm responsible for all those emotions, and most of them are not good.

At last, she releases a long exhale and hisses, "What you did hurt, Lucas. You wanted me to give myself to you just so you could tell me to screw off."

But that's not the case. I wanted her to give herself to me, so I could keep her. I was just too selfish and wrapped up in being with her to remember that Sam refused to let me enjoy even an ounce of happiness. My ex-wife's threat of taking me down and bringing Sienna along with me was so real.

Sienna clears her throat, ripping my thoughts away from Sam and back to her. "And now you want me again?" she demands, her voice breaking.

I tighten my grip around her because she's trembling but also because I am, too. "I've *always* wanted you. It just took me a while to tell the shit holding me back to fuck off."

"Sam?"

I nod. And when I told Sam that she was holding me back from living, she calmly agreed to back off—as long as I agreed to renegotiate the amount of money I pour into her accounts each month. Still, I decide to prepare Sienna for the worst because I know it's just a matter of time before Sam's calm facade disappears, giving way to her erratic demands and who knows what else.

I dip my face down until my nose touches the tip of Sienna's, which is damp from her tears. "If you're with me, she'll try to ruin me. She'll try to ruin you because she knows I love you. You've got to know that. You've got to know what she has on me—"

When she cuts me off by putting her fingers over my lips, I'm relieved. I'm relieved because I don't know what I should say next.

*You've got to know what she has on me would take me away from you, from my life as I know it, and I don't think there would be any going back.*

"Damn you, Lucas," Sienna says, but she's wearing a soft smile. Her hand slips from my mouth down to my neck, and I turn my head slightly to kiss her wrist. She shivers but doesn't let go of me.

"I know you're angry," I say. She'll probably be that way for a long time—months or maybe even years. "And I know that it'll take work, but I just want you to try to give getting through my fuck-ups together a chance. I need to know that you can give a shit about me again."

Her smile gradually disappears. For the longest damn minute of my life, her face is an emotionless mask. A hundred shitty thoughts roll through my brain before she incredulously moves her head to each side as she mumbles something that sounds like *dumbass*. She rests her head on my shoulder, and I can feel her tears seeping through my T-shirt. "A lot can happen in the two days I owe you, but you're right. You *are* an idiot if you thought I ever stopped loving you."

"I love you, too, Sienna," I growl. Then, my hands are all over her as I bring her mouth to mine. Her lips part willingly, and her tongue darts into my mouth. She tastes sweet—*so goddamn sweet*—and I swear I'll never lose the taste of her again.

I'll fight like hell to keep this woman beside me.

Sienna's eyes are still squeezed together when she pulls away, but when I press her hand up against my cock, they quickly open. She glances down our bodies before clearing her throat.

"If we weren't at your Grams' house…" I say.

Her mouth falls open in surprise. "She's not…" Sienna starts, but then she shakes her head and runs her palms nervously down the front of her shorts. "There are hotels just a couple of miles away from—"

"Come with me."

"What?"

I gesture up the driveway to where I parked the Audi. "Two days. I want those two days now." It's a bold-ass move on my part, but she doesn't immediately shoot it down.

Instead, she bites her bottom lip. "Right *now*?"

"Yeah," I say, stroking my thumb across her lips to stop her from nibbling them. Keeping her eyes focused on mine, she bites the tip of my finger, and I groan in frustration. *Why does she have to do shit like that?* "I'm sorry, Si, and I need a chance to fucking prove myself."

She nods, backing into the house and motioning for me to follow her, but I stay in the doorway. "I'll have to go pack my things," she tells me, pointing at the staircase six feet behind her.

"And I've got to call Grams. She's not here." Her face is flushed, and I can tell she's mentally making a list of what all needs to be done before she can come with me. Suddenly, she frowns. "Lucas, you're not going to—"

And there goes the pain in my chest again. She doesn't trust me, and it just about destroys me. *But what can I expect?*

"Nothing will happen to you while you're with me," I promise her. Then, I lift my eyebrows and add, "Nothing bad, that is. I'm going to do what I should've done before, and I'm not going to make you leave. That's the last thing I'd ask of you now."

It is that promise that completely wins her over.

She tugs me to her by the collar of my shirt and cups my face in between her hands. Her lips are rough and demanding, making me reconsider what she started to say earlier about all the nearby hotels. I drag myself away from her, putting a good amount of space between us.

"Give me an hour to get ready," she whispers, walking backward into the house. "I promise I won't be long." Her eyes don't leave mine until she turns to go up the steps, and my eyes don't leave her ass until she rounds the corner at the top of the staircase.

It only takes her a half an hour to come back outside. After I place her luggage into the trunk of the silver Audi, which I parked close to the cabin, Sienna slips into the passenger seat next to me. Dragging in a shaky breath, she places her head against the leather headrest and then turns to look at me as I put the car into drive.

"I love you, Lucas," she says.

"I love you, too."

When I stop at the end of the driveway, I produce a wide red scarf from the center console. The corners of her mouth slide into a smile.

"What's this for?" she questions as I cover her eyes with the fabric.

"Surprises are your new best friend, Sienna."

And to my surprise, she doesn't even protest.

# And look for *Consumed*, coming Fall 2013

# Acknowledgments

Thank you so much to my readers—to YOU—for being so amazing. Your enthusiasm and support for my books amaze me on a daily basis, and I feel so blessed to have you. Thank you for all the emails, reviews, and Facebook messages. You rock my world!

To Kelli Maine, Michelle Valentine, and Kristen Proby—You ladies constantly brighten my day, putting up with my randomness and making me laugh. I love you girls like a love song, and I can't WAIT to rock Vegas with you all! :)

Christine Bezdenejnih Estevez, you are one amazing chick! Thank you for keeping me organized and for loving my books. BIG HUGS for everything you do (and it's a lot)!

To Rebecca, my ass-kicking agent—Thank you for all your wisdom and support. You keep me sane!

To Jovana Shirley with Unforeseen Editing—You are so incredibly talented! Thank you for taking Savor You and marking it up with your red pen of greatness. I'm so grateful for all your insight and suggestions!

Thank you to my early readers: Lisa Kane, Lisa Rutledge, Tracey Kruger, Dawn Martens, Aimee Pachorek, Lourdes Sanchez, America Matthew, Kim Person, and Jennifer Wolfel. I appreciate you ladies so much for taking the time to read over my pages and for giving me insight. Your opinions are invaluable to me.

Thanks to Letitia Hasser at RBA Designs for creating such a beautiful book cover. Your artwork brings Kylie to life!

To Cris Hadarly, Becca Manuel, and Abbie Dauenheimer—Thank you ladies a million times for being so effing creative. I love the trailers and collages, and I smile like an idiot every time I look at them.

To the bloggers in the romance community—THANK YOU! Your support and love for my books mean so much to me. I appreciate you all more than you could ever imagine. Thank you for taking such good care of me and all the other indie authors!

And to my family—You guys rock my socks! (Don't look at my feet right now because they're mismatched.) Thanks for encouraging me to follow this dream of mine. I love you guys.

# ABOUT THE AUTHOR

Emily Snow is *The New York Times* and *USA Today* bestselling author of the *Devoured* series (October 2012, January 2013) and *Tidal* (December 2012). She loves books, sexy bad boys, and really loud rock music, so naturally, she writes stories about naughty rockers. Visit her blog at http://emilysnowbooks.blogspot.com and her website at www.emilysnowbooks.com for news, teasers, and contests.

Find Emily on **Twitter** @EmilySnowBks

See Emily's *Savor You* inspiration on **Pinterest**

Or

Follow and Friend Emily Snow on **Facebook**